THE BRIDE OF
THE MISTLETOE

JAMES LANE ALLEN

1st WORLD
LIBRARY
Literary Society

The Bride of the Mistletoe

James Lane Allen

© 1st World Library – Literary Society, 2004
PO Box 2211
Fairfield, IA 52556
www.1stworldlibrary.org
First Edition

LCCN: 2004195325

Softcover ISBN: 1-4218-0156-6
Hardcover ISBN: 1-4218-0056-X
eBook ISBN: 1-4218-0256-2

Purchase *"The Bride of the Mistletoe"*
as a traditional bound book at:
www.1stWorldLibrary.org/purchase.asp?ISBN=1-4218-0156-6

1st World Library Literary Society is a nonprofit
organization dedicated to promoting literacy by:

- Creating a free internet library accessible from any computer worldwide.
- Hosting writing competitions and offering book publishing scholarships.

The Bride of the Mistletoe
contributed by Tim, Ed & Rodney
in support of
1st World Library Literary Society

TO ONE WHO KNOWS

Je crois que pour produire il ne faut pas trop raissoner. Mais il faut regarder beaucoup et songer à ce qu'on a vu. Voir: tout est là, et voir juste. J'entends, par voir juste, voir avec ses propres yeux et non avec ceux des maîtres. L'originalité d'un artiste s'indique d'abord dans les petites choses et non dans les grandes.

Il faut trouver aux choses une signification qui n'a pas encore découverte et tâcher de l'exprimer d'une façon personelle.

GUY DE MAUPASSANT.

PREFACE

Any one about to read this work of fiction might properly be apprised beforehand that it is not a novel: it has neither the structure nor the purpose of The Novel.

It is a story. There are two characters - a middle-aged married couple living in a plain farmhouse; one point on the field of human nature is located; at that point one subject is treated; in the treatment one movement is directed toward one climax; no external event whatsoever is introduced; and the time is about forty hours.

A second story of equal length, laid in the same house, is expected to appear within a twelvemonth. The same father and mother are characters, and the family friend the country doctor; but subordinately all. The main story concerns itself with the four children of the two households.

It is an American children's story:

"A Brood of The Eagle."

During the year a third work, not fiction, will be published, entitled:

"The Christmas Tree: An Interpretation."

The three works will serve to complete each other, and they complete a cycle of the theme.

CONTENTS

EARTH SHIELD AND EARTH FESTIVAL

A mighty table-land lies southward in a hardy region of our country. It has the form of a colossal Shield, lacking and broken in some of its outlines and rough and rude of make. Nature forged it for some crisis in her long warfare of time and change, made use of it, and so left it lying as one of her ancient battle-pieces - Kentucky.

The great Shield is raised high out of the earth at one end and sunk deep into it at the other. It is tilted away from the dawn toward the sunset. Where the western dip of it reposes on the planet, Nature, cunning artificer, set the stream of ocean flowing past with restless foam - the Father of Waters. Along the edge for a space she bound a bright river to the rim of silver. And where the eastern part rises loftiest on the horizon, turned away from the reddening daybreak, she piled shaggy mountains wooded with trees that loose their leaves ere snowflakes fly and with steadfast evergreens which hold to theirs through the gladdening and the saddening year. Then crosswise over the middle of the Shield, northward and southward upon the breadth of it, covering the life-born rock of many thicknesses, she drew a tough skin of verdure - a broad strip of hide of the ever growing grass. She embossed noble forests on this greensward and under the forests drew clear waters.

This she did in a time of which we know nothing - uncharted ages before man had emerged from the deeps of ocean with eyes to wonder, thoughts to wander, heart to love, and spirit to pray. Many a scene the same power has wrought out upon the surface of the Shield since she brought him forth and set him there: many an old one, many a new. She has made it sometimes a Shield of war, sometimes a Shield of peace. Nor has she yet finished with its destinies as she has not yet finished with anything in the universe. While therefore she continues her will and pleasure elsewhere throughout creation, she does not forget the Shield.

She likes sometimes to set upon it scenes which admonish man how little his lot has changed since Hephaistos wrought like scenes upon the shield of Achilles, and Thetis of the silver feet sprang like a falcon from snowy Olympus bearing the glittering piece of armor to her angered son.

These are some of the scenes that were wrought on the shield of Achilles and that to-day are spread over the Earth Shield Kentucky:

Espousals and marriage feasts and the blaze of lights as they lead the bride from her chamber, flutes and violins sounding merrily. An assembly-place where the people are gathered, a strife having arisen about the blood-price of a man slain; the old lawyers stand up one after another and make their tangled arguments in turn. Soft, freshly ploughed fields where ploughmen drive their teams to and fro, the earth growing dark behind the share. The estate of a landowner where laborers are reaping; some armfuls the binders are binding with twisted bands of straw: among them the farmer is standing in silence, leaning on his staff, rejoicing in his heart. Vineyards with purpling clusters and happy folk gathering these in plaited baskets on sunny afternoons. A herd of cattle with incurved horns hurrying from the stable to the woods where there is running water and where purple-topped weeds bend above the sleek grass. A fair glen with white sheep. A dancing-place under the trees; girls and young men dancing, their fingers on one another's wrists: a great company stands watching the lovely dance of joy.

Such pageants appeared on the shield of Achilles as art; as pageants of life they appear on the Earth Shield Kentucky. The metal-worker of old wrought them upon the armor of the Greek warrior in tin and silver, bronze and gold. The world-designer sets them to-day on the throbbing land in nerve and blood, toil and delight and passion. But there with the old things she mingles new things, with the never changing the ever changing; for the old that remains always the new and the new that perpetually becomes old - these Nature allots to man as his two portions wherewith he must abide steadfast in what he is and go upward or go downward through all that he is to become.

But of the many scenes which she in our time sets forth upon the stately grassy Shield there is a single spectacle that she spreads over the length and breadth of it once every year now as best liked by the entire people; and this is both old and new.

It is old because it contains man's faith in his immortality, which was venerable with age before the shield of Achilles ever grew effulgent before the sightless orbs of Homer. It is new because it contains those latest hopes and reasons for this faith, which briefly blossom out upon the primitive stock with the altering years and soon are blown away upon the winds of change. Since this spectacle, this festival, is thus old and is thus new and thus enwraps the deepest thing in the human spirit, it is never forgotten.

When in vernal days any one turns a furrow or sows in the teeth of the wind and glances at the fickle sky; when under the summer shade of a flowering tree any one looks out upon his fatted herds and fattening grain; whether there is autumnal plenty in his barn or autumnal emptiness, autumnal peace in his breast or autumnal strife, - all days of the year, in the assembly-place, in the dancing-place, whatsoever of good or ill befall in mind or hand, never does one forget.

When nights are darkest and days most dark; when the sun seems farthest from the planet and cheers it with lowest heat; when the fields lie shorn between harvest-time and seed-time and man turns wistful eyes back and forth between the mystery of his origin and the mystery of his end, - then comes the great pageant of the winter solstice, then comes Christmas.

So what is Christmas? And what for centuries has it been to differing but always identical mortals?

It was once the old pagan festival of dead Nature. It was once the old pagan festival of the reappearing sun. It was the pagan festival when the hands of labor took their rest and hunger took its fill. It was the pagan festival to honor the descent of the fabled inhabitants of an upper world upon the earth, their commerce with common flesh, and the production of a race of divine-and-human half-breeds. It is now the festival of the Immortal Child appearing in the midst of mortal

James Lane Allen

children. It is now the new festival of man's remembrance of his errors and his charity toward erring neighbors. It has latterly become the widening festival of universal brotherhood with succor for all need and nighness to all suffering; of good will warring against ill will and of peace warring upon war.

And thus for all who have anywhere come to know it, Christmas is the festival of the better worldly self. But better than worldliness, it is on the Shield to-day what it essentially has been through many an age to many people - the symbolic Earth Festival of the Evergreen; setting forth man's pathetic love of youth - of his own youth that will not stay with him; and renewing his faith in a destiny that winds its ancient way upward out of dark and damp toward Eternal Light.

This is a story of the Earth Festival on the Earth Shield.

I. THE MAN AND THE SECRET

A man sat writing near a window of an old house out in the country a few years ago; it was afternoon of the twenty-third of December.

One of the volumes of a work on American Forestry lay open on the desk near his right hand; and as he sometimes stopped in his writing and turned the leaves, the illustrations showed that the long road of his mental travels - for such he followed - was now passing through the evergreens.

Many notes were printed at the bottoms of the pages. They burned there like short tapers in dim places, often lighting up obscure faiths and customs of our puzzled human race. His eyes roved from taper to taper, as gathering knowledge ray by ray. A small book lay near the large one. It dealt with primitive nature-worship; and it belonged in the class of those that are kept under lock and key by the libraries which possess them as unsafe reading for unsafe minds.

Sheets of paper covered with the man's clear, deliberate handwriting lay thickly on the desk. A table in the centre of the room was strewn with volumes, some of a secret character, opened for reference. On the tops of two bookcases and on the mantelpiece were prints representing scenes from the oldest known art of the East. These and other prints hanging about the walls, however remote from each other in the times and places where they had been gathered, brought together in this room of a quiet Kentucky farmhouse evidence bearing upon the same object: the subject related in general to trees and in especial evergreens.

While the man was immersed in his work, he appeared not to be submerged. His left hand was always going out to one or the other of three picture-frames on the desk and his fingers bent caressingly.

Two of these frames held photographs of four young children - a boy and a girl comprising each group. The children had the air of being well enough bred to be well behaved before the camera, but of being unruly and disorderly out of sheer health and a wild natural-ness. All of them looked straight at you; all had eyes wide open with American frankness and good humor; all had mouths shut tight with American energy and determination. Apparently they already believed that the New World was behind them, that the nation backed them up. In a way you believed it. You accepted them on the spot as embodying that marvellous precocity in American children, through which they early in life become conscious of the country and claim it their country and believe that it claims them. Thus they took on the distinction of being a squad detached only photographically from the rank and file of the white armies of the young in the New World, millions and millions strong, as they march, clear-eyed, clear-headed, joyous, magnificent, toward new times and new destinies for the nation and for humanity - a kinder knowledge of man and a kinder ignorance of God.

The third frame held the picture of a woman probably thirty years of age. Her features were without noticeable American characteristics. What human traits you saw depended upon what human traits you saw with.

The hair was dark and abundant, the brows dark and strong. And the lashes were dark and strong; and the eyes themselves, so thornily hedged about, somehow brought up before you a picture of autumn thistles - thistles that look out from the shadow of a rock. They had a veritable thistle quality and suggestiveness: gray and of the fields, sure of their experience in nature, freighted with silence.

Despite grayness and thorniness, however, you saw that they were in the summer of their life-bloom; and singularly above even their beauty of blooming they held what is rare in the eyes of either men or women - they held a look of being just.

The whole face was an oval, long, regular, high-bred. If the lower part had been hidden behind a white veil of the Orient (by that little bank of snow which is guardedly built in front of the overflowing desires of the mouth), the upper part would have given the impression of reserve, coldness, possibly of severity; yet ruled by that one look - the garnered wisdom, the tempering justice, of the eyes. The whole face being seen, the lower features altered the impression made by the upper ones; reserve became bettered into strength, coldness bettered into dignity, severity of intellect transfused into glowing nobleness of character. The look of virgin justice in her was perhaps what had survived from that white light of life which falls upon young children as from a receding sun and touches lingeringly their smiles and glances; but her mouth had

James Lane Allen

gathered its shadowy tenderness as she walked the furrows of the years, watching their changeful harvests, eating their passing bread.

A handful of some of the green things of winter lay before her picture: holly boughs with their bold, upright red berries; a spray of the cedar of the Kentucky yards with its rosary of piteous blue. When he had come in from out of doors to go on with his work, he had put them there - perhaps as some tribute. After all his years with her, many and strong, he must have acquired various tributes and interpretations; but to-day, during his walk in the woods, it had befallen him to think of her as holly which ripens amid snows and retains its brave freshness on a landscape of departed things. As cedar also which everywhere on the Shield is the best loved of forest-growths to be the companion of household walls; so that even the poorest of the people, if it does not grow near the spot they build in, hunt for it and bring it home: everywhere wife and cedar, wife and cedar, wife and cedar.

The photographs of the children grouped on each side of hers with heads a little lower down called up memories of Old World pictures in which cherubs smile about the cloud-borne feet of the heavenly Hebrew maid. Glowing young American mother with four healthy children as her gifts to the nation - this was the practical thought of her that riveted and held.

As has been said, they were in two groups, the children; a boy and girl in each. The four were of nearly the same age; but the faces of two were on a dimmer card in an older frame. You glanced at her again and persuaded yourself that the expression of motherhood which characterized her separated into two expressions (as behind a thin white cloud it is possible to watch another cloud of darker hue). Nearer in time was the countenance of a mother happy with happy offspring; further away the same countenance withdrawn a little into shadow - the face of the mother bereaved - mute and changeless.

The man, the worker, whom this little flock of wife and two surviving children now followed through the world as their leader, sat with his face toward his desk In a corner of the room; solidly squared before his undertaking, liking it, mastering it; seldom changing his position as the minutes passed, never nervously; with a quietude in him that was oftener in Southern gentlemen in quieter, more gentlemanly times. A low powerful figure with a pair of thick shoulders and tremendous limbs; filling the room with his vitality as a heavy passionate animal lying in a corner of a cage fills the space of the cage, so that you wait for it to roll over or get up on its feet and walk about that you may study its markings and get an inkling of its conquering nature.

Meantime there were hints of him. When he had come in, he had thrown his overcoat on a chair that stood near the table in the centre of the room and had dropped his hat upon his coat. It had slipped to the floor and now lay there - a low, soft black hat of a kind formerly much worn by young Southerners of the countryside, - especially on occasions when there was a spur of heat in their mood and going, - much the same kind that one sees on the heads of students in Rome in winter; light, warm, shaping itself readily to breezes from any quarter, to be doffed or donned as comfortable and negligible. It suggested that he had been a country boy in the land, still belonged to the

James Lane Allen

land, and as a man kept to its out-of-door habits and fashions. His shoes, one of which you saw at each side of his chair, were especially well made for rough-going feet to tramp in during all weathers.

A sack suit of dark blue serge somehow helped to withdraw your interpretation of him from farm life to the arts or the professions. The scrupulous air of his shirt collar, showing against the clear-hued flesh at the back of his neck, and the Van Dyck-like edge of the shirt cuff, defining his powerful wrist and hand, strengthened the notion that he belonged to the arts or to the professions. He might have been sitting before a canvas instead of a desk and holding a brush instead of a pen: the picture would have been true to life. Or truer yet, he might have taken his place with the grave group of students in the Lesson in Anatomy left by Rembrandt.

Once he put down his pen, wheeled his chair about, and began to read the page he had just finished: then you saw him. He had a big, masculine, solid-cut, self-respecting, normal-looking, executive head - covered with thick yellowish hair clipped short; so that while everything else in his appearance indicated that he was in the prime of manhood, the clipped hair caused him to appear still more youthful; and it invested him with a rustic atmosphere which went along very naturally with the sentimental country hat and the all-weather shoes. He seemed at first impression a magnificent animal frankly loved of the sun - perhaps too warmly. The sun itself seemed to have colored for him his beard and mustache - a characteristic hue of men's hair and beard in this land peopled from Old English stock. The beard, like the hair, was cut short, as though his idea might have been to get both hair and beard out of life's daily way; but his mustache curled thickly down over his mouth, hiding it. In the whole effect there was a suggestion of the Continent, perhaps of a former student career in Germany, memories of which may still have lasted with him and the marks of which may have purposely been kept up in his appearance.

But such a fashion of beard, while covering a man's face, does much to uncover the man. As he sat amid his papers and books, your thought surely led again to old pictures where earnest heads bend together over some point on the human road, at which knowledge widens and suffering begins to be made more bearable and death more kind. Perforce now you interpreted him and fixed his general working category: that he was absorbed in work meant to be serviceable to humanity. His house, the members of his family, the people of his neighborhood, were meantime forgotten: he was not a mere dweller on his farm; he was a discoverer on the wide commons where the race forever camps at large with its problems, joys, and sorrows.

He read his page, his hand dropped to his knee, his mind dropped its responsibility; one of those intervals followed when the brain rests. The look of the student left his face; over it began to play the soft lights of the domestic affections. He had forgotten the world for his own place in the world; the student had become the husband and house-father. A few moments only; then he wheeled gravely to his work again, his right hand took up the pen, his left hand went back to the pictures.

The silence of the room seemed a guarded silence, as though he were being watched over by a love which would not let him be disturbed. (He had the reposeful self-assurance of a man who is conscious that he is idolized.)

Matching the silence within was the stillness out of doors. An immense oak tree stood just outside the windows. It was a perpetual reminder of vanished woods; and when a windstorm tossed and twisted it, the straining and grinding of the fibres were like struggles and outcries for the wild life of old. This afternoon it brooded motionless, an image of forest reflection. Once a small black-and-white sapsucker, circling the trunk and peering into the crevices of the bark on a level with the windows, uttered minute notes which penetrated into the room like steel darts of sound. A snowbird alighted on the window-sill, glanced familiarly in at the man, and shot up its crest; but disappointed perhaps that it was not noticed, quoted its resigned gray phrase - a phrase it had made for itself to accompany the score of gray whiter - and flitted on billowy wings to a juniper at the corner of the house, its turret against the long javelins of the North.

Amid the stillness of Nature outside and the house-silence of a love guarding him within, the man worked on.

A little clock ticked independently on the old-fashioned Parian marble mantelpiece. Prints were propped against its sides and face, illustrating the use of trees about ancient tombs and temples. Out of this photographic grove of dead things the uncaring clock threw out upon the air a living three - the fateful three that had been measured for each tomb and temple in its own land and time.

A knock, regretful but positive, was heard, and the door opening into the hall was quietly pushed open. A glow lit up the student's face though he did not stop writing; and his voice, while it gave a welcome, unconsciously expressed regret at being disturbed:

"Come in."

"I am in!"

He lifted his heavy figure with instant courtesy - rather obsolete now - and bowing to one side, sat down again.

"So I see," he said, dipping his pen into his ink.

"Since you did not turn around, you would better have said 'So I hear.' It is three o'clock."

"So I hear."

"You said you would be ready."

"I am ready."

"You said you would be done."

"I am done - nearly done."

"How nearly?"

"By to-morrow - to-morrow afternoon before dark. I have reached the end, but now it is hard to stop, hard to let go."

His tone gave first place, primary consideration, to his work. The silence in the room suddenly became charged. When the voice was heard again, there was constraint in it:

"There is something to be done this afternoon before dark, something I have a share in. Having a share, I am interested. Being interested, I am prompt. Being prompt, I am here."

He waved his hand over the written sheets before him - those cold Alps of learning; and asked reproachfully:

"Are you not interested in all this, O you of little faith?"

"How can I say, O me of little knowledge!"

As the words impulsively escaped, he heard a quick movement behind him. He widened out his heavy arms upon his manuscript and looked back over his shoulder at her and laughed. And still smiling and holding his pen between his fingers, he turned and faced her. She had advanced into the middle of the room and had stopped at the chair on which he had thrown his overcoat and hat. She had picked up the hat and stood turning it and pushing its soft material back into shape for his head - without looking at him.

The northern light of the winter afternoon, entering through the looped crimson-damask curtains, fell side-wise upon the woman of the picture.

Years had passed since the picture had been made. There were changes in her; she looked younger. She had effaced the ravages of a sadder period of her life as human voyagers upon reaching quiet port repair the damages of wandering and storm. Even the look of motherhood, of the two motherhoods, which so characterized her in the photograph, had disappeared for the present. Seeing her now for the first time, one would have said that her whole mood and bearing made a single declaration: she was neither wife nor mother; she was a woman in love with life's youth - with youth - youth; in love with the things that youth alone could ever secure to her.

The carriage of her beautiful head, brave and buoyant, brought before you a vision of growing things in nature as they move towards their summer yet far away. There still was youth in the round white throat above the collar of green velvet - woodland green - darker than the green of the cloth she wore. You were glad she had chosen that color because she was going for a walk with him; and green would enchain the eye out on the sere ground and under the stripped trees. The flecklessness of her long gloves drew your thoughts to winter rather - to its one beauteous gift dropped from soiled clouds. A slender toque brought out the keenness in the oval of her face. From it rose one backward-sweeping feather of green shaded to coral at the tip; and there your fancy may have cared to see lingering the last radiance of whiter-sunset skies.

He kept his seat with his back to the manuscript from which he had repulsed her; and his eyes swept loyally over her as she waited. Though she could scarcely trust herself to speak, still less could she endure the silence. With her face turned toward the windows opening on the lawn, she stretched out her arm toward him and softly shook his hat at him.

"The sun sets - you remember how many minutes after four," she said, with no other tone than that of quiet warning. "I marked the minutes in the almanac for you the other night after the children had gone to bed, so that you would not forget. You know how short the twilights are even when the day is clear. It is cloudy to-day and there will not be any twilight. The children said they would not be at home until after dark, but they may come sooner; it may be a trick. They have threatened to catch us this year in one way or another, and you know they must not do that - not this year! There must be one more Christmas with all its old ways - even if it must be without its old mysteries."

He did not reply at once and then not relevantly:

"I heard you playing."

He had dropped his head forward and was scowling at her from under his brows with a big Beethoven brooding scowl. She did not see, for she held her face averted.

The silence in the room again seemed charged, and there was greater constraint in her voice when it was next heard:

"I had to play; you need not have listened."

"I had to listen; you played loud -"

"I did not know I was playing loud. I may have been trying to drown other sounds," she admitted.

"What other sounds?" His voice unexpectedly became inquisitorial: it was a frank thrust into the unknown.

"Discords - possibly."

"What discords?" His thrust became deeper.

She turned her head quickly and looked at him; a quiver passed across her lips and in her eyes there was noble anguish.

But nothing so arrests our speech when we are tempted to betray hidden trouble as to find ourselves face to face with a kind of burnished, radiant happiness. Sensitive eyes not more quickly close before a blaze of sunlight than the shadowy soul shuts her gates upon the advancing Figure of Joy.

It was the whole familiar picture of him now - triumphantly painted in the harmonies of life, masterfully toned to subdue its discords - that drove her back into herself. When she spoke next, she had regained the self-control which under his unexpected attack she had come near losing; and her words issued from behind the closed gates - as through a crevice of the closed gates:

"I was reading one of the new books that came the other day, the deep grave ones you sent for. It is written by a deep grave German, and it is worked out in the deep grave German way. The whole purpose of it is to show that any woman in the life of any man is merely - an Incident. She may be this to him, she may be that to him; for a briefer time, for a greater time; but all along and in the end, at bottom, she is to him - an Incident."

He did not take his eyes from hers and his smile slowly broadened.

"Were those the discords?" he asked gently.

She did not reply.

He turned in his chair and looking over his shoulder at her, he raised his arm and drew the point of his pen across the backs of a stack of magazines on top of his desk.

"Here is a work," he said, "not written by a German or by any other man, but by a woman whose race I do not know: here is a work the sole purpose of which is to prove that any man is merely an Incident in the life of any woman. He may be this to her, he may be that to her; for a briefer time, for a greater time; but all along and in the end, beneath everything else, he is to her - an Incident."

He turned and confronted her, not without a gleam of humor in his eyes.

"That did not trouble me," he said tenderly. "Those were not discords to me."

Her eyes rested on his face with inscrutable searching. She made no comment.

His own face grew grave. After a moment of debate with himself as to whether he should be forced to do a thing he would rather not do, he turned in his chair and laid down his pen as though separating himself from his work. Then he said, in a tone that ended playfulness:

"Do I not understand? Have I not understood all the time? For a year now I have been shutting myself up at spare hours in this room and at this work - without any explanation to you. Such a thing never occurred before in our lives. You have shared everything. I have relied upon you and I have needed you, and you have never failed me. And this apparently has been your reward - to be rudely shut out at last. Now you come in and I tell you that the work is done - quite finished - without a word to you about it. Do I not understand?" he repeated. "Have I not understood all along? It is true; outwardly as regards this work you have been - the Incident."

As he paused, she made a slight gesture with one hand as though she did not care for what he was saying and brushed away the fragile web of his words from before her eyes - eyes fixed on larger things lying clear before her in life's distance.

He went quickly on with deepening emphasis:

"But, comrade of all these years, battler with me for life's victories, did you think you were never to know? Did you believe I was never to explain? You had only one more day to wait! If patience, if faith, could only have lasted another twenty-four hours - until Christmas Eve!"

It was the first time for nearly a year that the sound of those words had been heard in that house. He bent earnestly over toward her; he leaned heavily forward with his hands on his knees and searched her features with loyal chiding.

"Has not Christmas Eve its mysteries?" he asked, "its secrets for you and me? Think of Christmas Eve for you and me! Remember!"

Slowly as in a windless woods on a winter day a smoke from a woodchopper's smouldering fire will wander off and wind itself about the hidden life-buds of a young tree, muffling it while the atmosphere near by is clear, there now floated into the room to her the tender haze of old pledges and vows and of things unutterably sacred.

He noted the effect of his words and did not wait. He turned to his desk and, gathering up the sprigs of holly and cedar, began softly to cover her picture with them.

"Stay blinded and bewildered there," he said, "until the hour comes when holly and cedar will speak: on Christmas Eve you will understand; you will then see whether in this work you have been - the Incident."

Even while they had been talking the light of the short winter afternoon had perceptibly waned in the room.

She glanced through the windows at the darkening lawn; her eyes were tear-dimmed; to her it looked darker than it was. She held his hat up between her arms, making an arch for him to come and stand under.

"It is getting late," she said in nearly the same tone of quiet warning with which she had spoken before. "There is no time to lose."

He sprang up, without glancing behind him at his desk with its interrupted work, and came over and placed himself under the arch of her arms, looking at her reverently.

But his hands did not take hold, his arms hung down at his sides - the hands that were life, the arms that were love.

She let her eyes wander over his clipped tawny hair

and pass downward over his features to the well-remembered mouth under its mustache. Then, closing her quivering lips quickly, she dropped the cat softly on his head and walked toward the door. When she reached it, she put out one of her hands delicately against a panel and turned her profile over her shoulder to him:

"Do you know what is the trouble with both of those books?" she asked, with a struggling sweetness in her voice.

He had caught up his overcoat and as he put one arm through the sleeve with a vigorous thrust, he laughed out with his mouth behind the collar:

"I think I know what is the trouble with the authors of the books."

"The trouble is," she replied, "the trouble is that the authors are right and the books are right: men and women *are* only Incidents to each other in life," and she passed out into the hall.

"Human life itself for that matter is only an incident in the universe," he replied, "if we cared to look at it in that way; but we'd better not!"

He was standing near the table in the middle of the room; he suddenly stopped buttoning his overcoat. His eyes began to wander over the books, the prints, the pictures, embracing in a final survey everything that he had brought together from such distances of place and time. His work was in effect done. A sense of regret, a rush of loneliness, came over him as it comes upon all of us who reach the happy ending of toil that we have put our heart and strength in.

"Are you coming?" she called faintly from the hall.

"I am coming," he replied, and moved toward the door; but there he stopped again and looked back.

Once more there came into his face the devotion of the student; he was on the commons where the race encamps; he was brother to all brothers who join work to work for common good. He was feeling for the moment that through his hands ran the long rope of the world at which men - like a crew of sailors - tug at the Ship of Life, trying to tow her into some divine haven.

His task was ended. Would it be of service? Would it carry any message? Would it kindle in American homes some new light of truth, with the eyes of mothers and fathers fixed upon it, and innumerable children of the future the better for its shining?

"Are you coming?" she called more quiveringly.

"I am coming," he called back, breaking away from his revery, and raising his voice so it would surely reach her.

II. THE TREE AND THE SUNSET

She had quitted the house and, having taken a few steps across the short frozen grass of the yard as one walks lingeringly when expecting to be joined by a companion, she turned and stood with her eyes fixed on the doorway for his emerging figure.

"To-morrow night," he had said, smiling at her with one meaning in his words, "to-morrow night you will understand."

"Yes," she now said to herself, with another meaning in hers, "to-morrow night I must understand. Until to-morrow night, then, blinded and bewildered with holly and cedar let me be! Kind ignorance, enfold me and spare me! All happiness that I can control or conjecture, come to me and console me!"

And over herself she dropped a vesture of joy to greet him when he should step forth.

It was a pleasant afternoon to be out of doors and to go about what they had planned; the ground was scarcely frozen, there was no wind, and the whole sky was overcast with thin gray cloud that betrayed no movement. Under this still dome of silvery-violet light stretched the winter land; it seemed ready and waiting for its great festival.

James Lane Allen

The lawn sloped away from the house to a brook at the bottom, and beyond the brook the ground rose to a woodland hilltop. Across the distance you distinguished there the familiar trees of blue-grass pastures: white ash and black ash; white oak and red oak; white walnut and black walnut; and the scaly-bark hickory in his roughness and the sycamore with her soft leoparded limbs. The black walnut and the hickory brought to mind autumn days when children were abroad, ploughing the myriad leaves with booted feet and gathering their harvest of nuts - primitive food-storing instinct of the human animal still rampant in modern childhood: these nuts to be put away in garret and cellar and but scantily eaten until Christmas came.

Out of this woods on the afternoon air sounded the muffled strokes of an axe cutting down a black walnut partly dead; and when this fell, it would bring down with it bunches of mistletoe, those white pearls of the forest mounted on branching jade. To-morrow eager fingers would be gathering the mistletoe to decorate the house. Near by was a thicket of bramble and cane where, out of reach of cattle, bushes of holly thrived: the same fingers would be gathering that.

Bordering this woods on one side lay a cornfield. The corn had just been shucked, and beside each shock of fodder lay its heap of ears ready for the gathering wagon. The sight of the corn brought freshly to remembrance the red-ambered home-brew of the land which runs in a genial torrent through all days and nights of the year - many a full-throated rill - but never with so inundating a movement as at this season. And the same grain suggested also the smokehouses of all farms, in which larded porkers, fattened by it, had taken on posthumous honors as home-cured hams; and in which up under the black rafters home-made sausages were being smoked to their needed flavor over well-chosen chips.

Around one heap of ears a flock of home-grown turkeys, red-mottled, rainbow-necked, were feeding for their fate.

On the other side of the woods stretched a wheat-field, in the stubble of which coveys of bob-whites were giving themselves final plumpness for the table by picking up grains of wheat which had dropped into the drills at harvest time or other seeds which had ripened in the autumn aftermath.

Farther away on the landscape there was a hemp-field where hemp-breakers were making a rattling reedy music; during these weeks wagons loaded with the gold-bearing fibre begin to move creaking to the towns, helping to fill the farmer's pockets with holiday largess.

Thus everything needed for Christmas was there in sight: the mistletoe - the holly - the liquor of the land for the cups of hearty men - the hams and the sausages of fastidious housewives - the turkey and the quail - and crops transmutable into coin. They were in sight there - the fair maturings of the sun now ready to be turned into offerings to the dark solstice, the low activities of the soil uplifted to human joyance.

One last thing completed the picture of the scene.

The brook that wound across the lawn at its bottom was frozen to-day and lay like a band of jewelled samite trailed through the olive verdure. Along its margin evergreens grew. No pine nor spruce nor larch nor fir is native to these portions of the Shield; only the wild cedar, the shapeless and the shapely, belongs there. This assemblage of evergreens was not, then, one of the bounties of Nature; they had been planted.

It was the slender tapering spires of these evergreens with their note of deathless spring that mainly caught the eye on the whole landscape this dead winter day. Under the silvery-violet light of the sky they waited in beauty and in peace: the pale green of larch and spruce which seems always to go with the freshness of dripping Aprils; the dim blue-gray of pines which rather belongs to far-vaulted summer skies; and the dark green of firs - true comfortable winter coat when snows sift mournfully and icicles are spearing earthward.

These evergreens likewise had their Christmas meaning and finished the picture of the giving earth. Unlike the other things, they satisfied no appetite, they were ministers to no passions; but with them the Christmas of the intellect began: the human heart was to drape their boughs with its gentle poetry; and from their ever living spires the spiritual hope of humanity would take its flight toward the eternal.

Thus then the winter land waited for the oncoming of that strange travelling festival of the world which has roved into it and encamped gypsy-like from old lost countries: the festival that takes toll of field and wood, of hoof and wing, of cup and loaf; but that, best of all, wrings from the nature of man its reluctant tenderness for his fellows and builds out of his lonely doubts regarding this life his faith in a better one.

And central on this whole silent scene - the highest element in it - its one winter-red passion flower - the motionless woman waiting outside the house.

At last he came out upon the step.

He cast a quick glance toward the sky as though his first thought were of what the weather was going to be. Then as he buttoned the top button of his overcoat and pressed his bearded chin down over it to make it more comfortable under his short neck, with his other hand he gave a little pull at his hat - the romantic country hat; and he peeped out from under the rustic brim at her, smiling with old gayeties and old fondnesses. He bulked so rotund inside his overcoat and looked so short under the flat headgear that her first thought was how slight a disguise every year turned him into a good family Santa Claus; and she smiled back at him with the same gayeties and fondnesses of days gone by. But such a deeper pang pierced her that she turned away and walked hurriedly down the hill toward the evergreens.

He was quickly at her side. She could feel how animal youth in him released itself the moment he had come into the open air. There was brutal vitality in the way his shoes crushed the frozen ground; and as his overcoat sleeve rubbed against her arm, there was the same leaping out of life, like the rubbing of tinder against tinder. Halfway down the lawn he halted and laid his hand heavily on her wrist.

"Listen to that!" he said. His voice was eager, excited, like a boy's.

On the opposite side of the house, several hundred

yards away, the country turnpike ran; and from this there now reached them the rumbling of many vehicles, hurrying in close procession out of the nearest town and moving toward smaller villages scattered over the country; to its hamlets and cross-roads and hundreds of homes richer or poorer - every vehicle Christmas-laden: sign and foretoken of the Southern Yule-tide. There were matters and usages in those American carriages and buggies and wagons and carts the history of which went back to the England of the Georges and the Stuarts and the Henrys; to the England of Elizabeth, to the England of Chaucer; back through robuster Saxon times to the gaunt England of Alfred, and on beyond this till they were lost under the forest glooms of Druidical Britain.

They stood looking into each other's eyes and gathering into their ears the festal uproar of the turnpike. How well they knew what it all meant - this far-flowing tide of bounteousness! How perfectly they saw the whole picture of the town out of which the vehicles had come: the atmosphere of it already darkened by the smoke of soft coal pouring from its chimneys, so that twilight in it had already begun to fall ahead of twilight out in the country, and lamp-posts to glimmer along the little streets, and shops to be illuminated to the delight of window-gazing, mystery-loving children - wild with their holiday excitements and secrecies. Somewhere in the throng their own two children were busy unless they had already started home.

For years he had held a professorship in the college in this town, driving in and out from his home; but with the close of this academic year he was to join the slender file of Southern men who have been called to

Northern universities: this change would mean the end of life here. Both thought of this now - of the last Christmas in the house; and with the same impulse they turned their gaze back to it.

More than half a century ago the one starved genius of the Shield, a writer of songs, looked out upon the summer picture of this land, its meadows and ripening corn tops; and as one presses out the spirit of an entire vineyard when he bursts a solitary grape upon his tongue, he, the song writer, drained drop by drop the wine of that scene into the notes of a single melody. The nation now knows his song, the world knows it - the only music that has ever captured the joy and peace of American home life - embodying the very soul of it in the clear amber of sound.

This house was one of such homesteads as the genius sang of: a low, old-fashioned, brown-walled, gray-shingled house; with chimneys generous, with green window-shutters less than green and white window-sills less than white; with feudal vines giving to its walls their summery allegiance; not young, not old, but standing in the middle years of its strength and its honors; not needy, not wealthy, but answering Agar's prayer for neither poverty nor riches.

The two stood on the darkening lawn, looking back at it.

It had been the house of his fathers. He had brought her to it as his own on the afternoon of their wedding several miles away across the country. They had arrived at dark; and as she had sat beside him in the carriage, one of his arms around her and his other hand enfolding both of hers, she had first caught sight of it

James Lane Allen

through the forest trees - waiting for her with its lights just lit, its warmth, its privacies: and that had been Christmas Eve!

For her wedding day had been Christmas Eve. When she had announced her choice of a day, they had chidden her. But with girlish wilfulness she had clung to it the more positively.

"It is the most beautiful night of the year!" she had replied, brushing their objection aside with that reason alone. "And it is the happiest! I will be married on that night, when I am happiest!"

Alone and thinking it over, she had uttered other words to herself - yet scarce uttered them, rather felt them:

"Of old it was written how on Christmas Night the Love that cannot fail us became human. My love for him, which is the divine thing in my life and which is never to fail him, shall become human to him on that night."

When the carriage had stopped at the front porch, he had led her into the house between the proud smiling servants of his establishment ranged at a respectful distance on each side; and without surrendering her even to her maid - a new spirit of silence on him - he had led her to her bedroom, to a place on the carpet under the chandelier.

Leaving her there, he had stepped backward and surveyed her waiting in her youth and loveliness - *for him;* come into his house, into his arms - *his*; no other's - never while life lasted to be another's even in thought or in desire.

Then as if the marriage ceremony of the afternoon in the presence of many had meant nothing and this were the first moment when he could gather her home to him, he had come forward and taken her in his arms and set upon her the kiss of his house and his ardor and his duty. As his warm breath broke close against her face, his lips under their mustache, almost boyish then, had thoughtlessly formed one little phrase - one little but most lasting and fateful phrase:

"Bride of the Mistletoe!"

Looking up with a smile, she saw that she stood under a bunch of mistletoe swung from the chandelier.

Straightway he had forgotten his own words, nor did he ever afterwards know that he had used them. But she, out of their very sacredness as the first words he had spoken to her in his home, had remembered them most clingingly. More than remembered them: she had set them to grow down into the fibres of her heart as the mistletoe roots itself upon the life-sap of the tree. And in all the later years they had been the green spot of verdure under life's dark skies - the undying bough into which the spirit of the whole tree retreats from the ice of the world:

"Bride of the Mistletoe!"

Through the first problem of learning to weld her nature to his wisely; through the perils of bearing children and the agony of seeing some of them pass away; through the ambition of having him rise in his profession and through the ideal of making his home an earthly paradise; through loneliness when he was away and joy whenever he came back, - upon her whole life had rested the wintry benediction of that mystical phrase:

"*Bride of the Mistletoe!*"

*   *   *   *   *

She turned away now, starting once more downward toward the evergreens. He was quickly at her side.

"What do you suppose Harold and Elizabeth are up to about this time?" he asked, with a good-humored jerk of his head toward the distant town.

"At least to something mischievous, whatever it is," she replied. "They begged to be allowed to stay until the shop windows were lighted; they have seen the shop windows two or three times already this week: there is no great marvel for them now in shop windows. Permission to stay late may be a blind to come home early. They are determined, from what I have overheard, to put an end this year to the parental house mysteries of Christmas. They are crossing the boundary between the first childhood and the second. But if it be possible, I wish everything to be kept once more just as it has always been; let it be so for my sake!"

"And I wish it for your sake," he replied heartily; "and for my purposes."

After a moment of silence he asked: "How large a Tree must it be this year?"

"It will have to be large," she replied; and she began to count those for whom the Tree this year was meant.

First she called the names of the two children they had lost. Gifts for these were every year hung on the boughs. She mentioned their names now, and then she continued counting:

"Harold and Elizabeth are four. You and I make six. After the family come Herbert and Elsie, your best friend the doctor's children. Then the servants - long strong bottom branches for the servants! Allow for the other children who are to make up the Christmas party: ten children have been invited, ten children have accepted, ten children will arrive. The ten will bring with them some unimportant parents; you can judge."

"That will do for size," he said, laughing. "Now the kind: spruce - larch - hemlock - pine - which shall it be?"

"It shall be none of them!" she answered, after a little waiting. "It shall be the Christmas Tree of the uttermost North where the reindeer are harnessed and the Great White Sleigh starts - fir. The old Christmas stories like fir best. Old faiths seem to lodge in it longest. And deepest mystery darkens the heart of it," she added.

"Fir it shall be!" he said. "Choose the tree."

"I have chosen."

She stopped and delicately touched his wrist with the finger tips of one white-gloved hand, bidding him stand beside her.

"That one," she said, pointing down.

The brook, watering the roots of the evergreens in summer gratefully, but now lying like a band of samite, jewel-crusted, made a loop near the middle point of the lawn, creating a tiny island; and on this island, aloof from its fellows and with space for the growth of its boughs, stood a perfect fir tree: strong-based, thick-set, tapering faultlessly, star-pointed, gathering more youth as it gathered more years - a tame dweller on the lawn but descended from forests blurred with wildness and lapped by low washings of the planet's primeval ocean.

At each Christmas for several years they had been tempted to cut this tree, but had spared it for its conspicuous beauty at the edge of the thicket.

"That one," she now said, pointing down. "This is the last time. Let us have the best of things while we may! Is it not always the perfect that is demanded for sacrifice?"

His glance had already gone forward eagerly to the tree, and he started toward it.

Descending, they stepped across the brook to the island and went up close to the fir. With a movement not unobserved by her he held out his hand and clasped three green fingers of a low bough which the fir seemed to stretch out to him recognizingly. (She had always realized the existence of some intimate bond between him and the forest.) His face now filled with meanings she did not share; the spell of the secret work had followed him out of the house down to the trees; incommunicable silence shut him in. A moment later his fingers parted with the green fingers of the fir and he moved away from her side, starting around the tree and studying it as though in delight of fresh knowledge. So she watched him pass around to the other side.

When he came back where he had started, she was not there. He looked around searchingly; her figure was nowhere in sight.

He stood - waiting.

The valley had memories, what memories! The years came close together here; they clustered as thickly as the trees themselves. Vacant spots among them marked where the Christmas Trees of former years had been cut down. Some of the Trees had been for the two children they had lost. This wandering trail led hither and thither back to the first Tree for the first child: he had stooped down and cut that close to the ground with his mere penknife. When it had been lighted, it had held only two or three candles; and the candle on the top of it had flared level into the infant's hand-shaded eyes.

He knew that she was making through the evergreens a Pilgrimage of the Years, walking there softly and alone with the feet of life's Pities and a mother's Constancies.

He waited for her - motionless.

The stillness of the twilight rested on the valley now. Only from the trees came the plaintive twittering of birds which had come in from frozen weeds and fence-rows and at the thresholds of the boughs were calling to one another. It was not their song, but their speech; there was no love in it, but there was what for them perhaps corresponds to our sense of ties. It most

James Lane Allen

resembled in human life the brief things that two people, having long lived together, utter to each other when together in a room they prepare for the night: there is no anticipation; it is a confession of the unconfessed. About him now sounded this low winter music from the far boundary of other lives.

He did not hear it.

The light on the landscape had changed. The sun was setting and a splendor began to spread along the sky and across the land. It laid a glory on the roof of the house on the hill; it smote the edge of the woodland pasture, burnishing with copper the gray domes; it shone faintly on distant corn shocks, on the weather-dark tents of the hemp at bivouac soldierly and grim. At his feet it sparkled in rose gleams on the samite of the brook and threw burning shafts into the gloom of the fir beside him.

He did not see it.

He did not hear the calling of the birds about his ears, he did not see the sunset before his eyes, he did not feel the fir tree the boughs of which stuck against his side.

He stood there as still as a rock - with his secret. Not the secret of the year's work, which was to be divulged to his wife and through her to the world; but the secret which for some years had been growing in his life and which would, he hoped, never grow into the open - to be seen of her and of all men.

The sentimental country hat now looked as though it might have been worn purposely to help out a disguise, as the more troubled man behind the scenes makes up to be the happier clown. It became an absurdity, a mockery, above his face grave, stern, set of jaw and eye. He was no longer the student buried among his books nor human brother to toiling brothers. He had not the slightest thought of service to mankind left in him, he was but a man himself with enough to think of in the battle between his own will and blood.

And behind him among the dark evergreens went on that Pilgrimage of the Years - with the feet of the Pities and the Constancies.

Moments passed; he did not stir. Then there was a slight noise on the other side of the tree, and his nature instantly stepped back into his outward place. He looked through the boughs. She had returned and was standing with her face also turned toward the sunset; it was very pale, very still.

Such darkness had settled on the valley now that the green she wore blent with the green of the fir. He saw only her white face and her white hands so close to the branches that they appeared to rest upon them, to grow out of them: he sadly thought of one of his prints of Egypt of old and of the Lady of the Sacred Tree. Her long backward-sweeping plume of green also blent with the green of the fir - shade to shade - and only the coral tip of it remained strongly visible. This matched the last coral in the sunset; and it seemed to rest ominously above her head as a finger-point of the fading light of Nature.

He went quickly around to her. He locked his arms around her and drew her close and held her close; and thus for a while the two stood, watching the flame on the altar of the world as it sank lower, leaving emptiness and ashes.

Once she put out a hand and with a gesture full of majesty and nobleness waved farewell to the dying fire.

Still without a word he took his arms from around her and turned energetically to the tree.

He pressed the lowest boughs aside and made his way in close to the trunk and struck it with a keen stroke.

The fir as he drew the axe out made at its gashed throat a sound like that of a butchered, blood-strangled creature trying to cry out too late against a treachery. A horror ran through the boughs; the thousands of leaves were jarred by the death-strokes; and the top of it rocked like a splendid plume too rudely treated in a storm. Then it fell over on its side, bridging blackly the white ice of the brook.

Stooping, he lifted it triumphantly. He set the butt-end on one of his shoulders and, stretching his arms up, grasped the trunk and held the tree straight in the air, so that it seemed to be growing out of his big shoulder as out of a ledge of rock. Then he turned to her and laughed out in his strength and youth. She laughed joyously back at him, glorying as he did.

With a robust re-shouldering of the tree to make it more comfortable to carry, he turned and started up the hill toward the house. As she followed behind, the old mystery of the woods seemed at last to have taken bodily possession of him. The fir was riding on his shoulder, its arms met fondly around his neck, its fingers were caressing his hair. And it whispered back jeeringly to her through the twilight:

"Say farewell to him! He was once yours; he is yours no longer. He dandles the child of the forest on his shoulder instead of his children by you in the house. He belongs to Nature; and as Nature calls, he will always follow - though it should lead over the precipice or into the flood. Once Nature called him to you: remember how he broke down barriers until he won you. Now he is yours no longer - say good-by to him!"

With an imbued terror and desolation, she caught up with him. By a movement so soft that he should not be aware, she plucked him by the coat sleeve on the other side from the fir and held on to him as he strode on in careless joy.

Halfway up the hill lights began to flash from the windows of the house: a servant was bringing in the lamps. It was at this hour, in just this way, that she had first caught sight of them on that Christmas Eve when he had brought her home after the wedding.

She hurried around in front of him, wishing to read the expression of his eyes by the distant gleams from the windows. Would they have nothing to say to her about those winter twilight lamps? Did he, too, not remember?

His head and face were hidden; a thousand small spears of Nature bristled between him and her; but he laughed out to her from behind the rampart of the green spears.

At that moment a low sound in the distance drew her attention, and instantly alert she paused to listen. Then, forgetting everything else, she called to him with a rush of laughter like that of her mischief-loving girlhood:

"Quick! There they are! I heard the gate shut at the turnpike! They must not catch us! Quick! Quick!"

"Hurry, then!" he cried, as he ran forward, joining his laughter to hers. "Open the door for me!"

After this the night fell fast. The only sounds to be heard in the valley were the minute readjustments of the ice of the brook as it froze tighter and the distressed cries of the birds that had roosted in the fir.

So the Tree entered the house.

III. THE LIGHTING OF THE CANDLES

During the night it turned bitter cold. When morning came the sky was a turquoise and the wind a gale. The sun seemed to give out light but not heat - to lavish its splendor but withhold its charity. Moist flesh if it chanced to touch iron froze to it momentarily. So in whiter land the tongue of the ermine freezes to the piece of greased metal used as a trap and is caught and held there until the trapper returns or until it starves - starves with food on its tongue.

The ground, wherever the stiff boots of a farmhand struck it, resisted as rock. In the fetlocks of farm horses, as they moved shivering, balls of ice rattled like shaken tacks. The little roughnesses of woodland paths snapped off beneath the slow-searching hoofs of fodder-seeking cattle like points of glass.

Within their wool the sheep were comforted.

On higher fields which had given back their moisture to the atmosphere and now were dry, the swooping wind lifted the dust at intervals and dragged it away in flaunting yellow veils. The picture it made, being so ill-seasoned, led you to think of August drought when the grasshopper stills itself in the weeds and the smell of grass is hot in the nostrils and every bird holds its beak open and its wings lifted like cooling lattices

James Lane Allen

alongside its breast. In these veils of dust swarms of frost crystals sported - dead midgets of the dead North. Except crystal and dust and wind, naught moved out there; no field mouse, no hare nor lark nor little shielded dove. In the naked trees of the pasture the crow kept his beak as unseen as the owl's; about the cedars of the yard no scarlet feather warmed the day.

The house on the hill - one of the houses whose spirit had been blown into the amber of the poet's song - sent festal smoke out of its chimneys all day long. At intervals the radiant faces of children appeared at the windows, hanging wreaths of evergreens; or their figures flitted to and fro within as they wove garlands on the walls for the Christmas party. At intervals some servant with head and shoulders muffled in a bright-colored shawl darted trippingly from the house to the cabins in the yard and from the cabins back to the house - the tropical African's polar dance between fire and fire. By every sign it gave the house showed that it was marshalling its whole happiness.

One thing only seemed to make a signal of distress from afar. The oak tree beside the house, whose roots coiled warmly under the hearth-stones and whose boughs were outstretched across the roof, seemed to writhe and rock in its winter sleep with murmurings and tossings like a human dreamer trying to get rid of an unhappy dream. Imagination might have said that some darkest tragedy of forests long since gone still lived in this lone survivor - that it struggled to give up the grief and guilt of an ancient forest shame.

The weather moderated in the afternoon. A warm current swept across the upper atmosphere, developing everywhere behind it a cloud; and toward sundown out of this cloud down upon the Shield snow began to fall. Not the large wet flakes which sometimes descend too late in spring upon the buds of apple orchards; nor those mournfuller ones which drop too soon on dim wild violets in November woods, but winter snow, stern sculptor of Arctic solitudes.

*　*　*　*　*

It was Christmas Eve. It was snowing all over the Shield.

Softly the snow fell upon the year's footprints and pathways of children and upon schoolhouses now closed and riotously deserted. More softly upon too crowded asylums for them: houses of noonday darkness where eyes eagerly look out at the windows but do not see; houses of soundlessness where ears listen and do not hear any noise; houses of silence where lips try to speak but utter no word.

The snow of Christmas Eve was falling softly on the old: whose eyes are always seeing vanished faces, whose ears hear voices gentler than any the earth now knows, whose hands forever try to reach other hands vainly held out to them. Sad, sad to those who remember loved ones gone with their kindnesses the snow of Christmas Eve!

But sadder yet for those who live on together after kindnesses have ceased, or whose love went like a summer wind. Sad is Christmas Eve to them! Dark its snow and blinding!

*　*　*　*　*

It was late that night.

She came into the parlor, clasping the bowl of a shaded lamp - the only light in the room. Her face, always calm in life's wisdom, but agitated now by the tide of deep things coming swiftly in toward her, rested clear-cut upon the darkness.

She placed the lamp on a table near the door and seated herself beside it. But she pushed the lamp away unconsciously as though the light of the house were no longer her light; and she sat in the chair as though it were no longer her chair; and she looked about the room as though it were no longer hers nor the house itself nor anything else that she cared for most.

Earlier in the evening they had finished hanging the presents on the Tree; but then an interruption had followed: the children had broken profanely in upon them, rending the veil of the house mysteries; and for more than an hour the night had been given up to them. Now the children were asleep upstairs, already dreaming of Christmas Morn and the rush for the stockings. The servants had finished their work and were gone to their quarters out in the yard. The doors of the house were locked. There would be no more intrusion now, no possible interruption; all the years were to meet him and her - alone. For Life is the master dramatist: when its hidden tragedies are ready to utter themselves, everything superfluous quits the stage; it is the essential two who fill it! And how little the rest of the world ever hears of what takes place between the two!

A little while before he had left the room with the step-ladder; when he came back, he was to bring with him the manuscript - the silent snowfall of knowledge which had been deepening about him for a year. The time had already passed for him to return, but he did not come. Was there anything in the forecast of the night that made him falter? Was he shrinking - *him* shrink? She put away the thought as a strange outbreak of injustice.

How still it was outside the house with the snow falling! How still within! She began to hear the ticking of the tranquil old clock under the stairway out in the hall - always tranquil, always tranquil. And then she began to listen to the disordered strokes of her own heart - that red Clock in the body's Tower whose beats are sent outward along the streets and alleys of the blood; whose law it is to be alternately wound too fast by the fingers of Joy, too slow by the fingers of Sorrow; and whose fate, if it once run down, never afterwards either by Joy or Sorrow to be made to run again.

At last she could hear the distant door of his study open and close and his steps advance along the hall. With what a splendid swing and tramp he brought himself toward her! - with what self-unconsciousness and virile strength in his feet! His steps entered and crossed his bedroom, entered and crossed her bedroom; and then he stood there before her in the parlor doorway, a few yards off - stopped and regarded her intently, smiling.

In a moment she realized what had delayed him. When he had gone away with the step-ladder, he had on a well-worn suit in which, behind locked doors, he had been working all the afternoon at the decorations of the Tree. Now he came back ceremoniously dressed; the rest of the night was to be in her honor.

James Lane Allen

It had always been so on this anniversary of their bridal night. They had always dressed for it; the children now in their graves had been dressed for it; the children in bed upstairs were regularly dressed for it; the house was dressed for it; the servants were dressed for it; the whole life of that establishment had always been made to feel by honors and tendernesses and gayeties that this was the night on which he had married her and brought her home.

As her eyes swept over him she noted quite as never before how these anniversaries had not taken his youth away, but had added youth to him; he had grown like the evergreen in the middle of the room - with increase of trunk and limbs and with larger tides of strength surging through him toward the master sun. There were no ravages of married life in him. Time had merely made the tree more of a tree and made his youth more youth.

She took in momentary details of his appearance: a moisture like summer heat along the edge of his yellow hair, started by the bath into which he had plunged; the freshness of the enormous hands holding the manuscript; the muscle of the forearm bulging within the dress-coat sleeve. Many a time she had wondered how so perfect an animal as he had ever climbed to such an elevation of work; and then had wondered again whether any but such an animal ever in life does so climb - shouldering along with him the poise and breadth of health and causing the hot sun of the valley to shine on the mountain tops.

Finally she looked to see whether he, thus dressed in her honor, thus but the larger youth after all their years together, would return her greeting with a light in his eyes that had always made them so beautiful to her - a light burning as at a portal opening inward for her only.

His eyes rested on his manuscript.

He brought it wrapped and tied in the true holiday spirit - sprigs of cedar and holly caught in the ribands; and he now lifted and held it out to her as a jeweller might elevate a casket of gems. Then he stepped forward and put it on the table at her elbow.

"For you!" he said reverently, stepping back.

There had been years when, returning from a tramp across the country, he would bring her perhaps nothing but a marvellous thistle, or a brilliant autumn leaf for her throat.

"For you!" he would say; and then, before he could give it to her, he would throw it away and take her in his arms. Afterwards she would pick up the trifle and treasure it.

"For you!" he now said, offering her the treasure of his year's toil and stepping back.

So the weight of the gift fell on her heart like a stone. She did not look at it or touch it but glanced up at him. He raised his finger, signalling for silence; and going to the chimney corner, brought back a long taper and held it over the lamp until it ignited. Then with a look which invited her to follow, he walked to the Tree and began to light the candles.

He began at the lowest boughs and, passing around,

James Lane Allen

touched them one by one. Around and around he went, and higher and higher twinkled the lights as they mounted the tapering sides of the fir. At the top he kindled one highest red star, shining down on everything below. Then he blew out the taper, turned out the lamp; and returning to the tree, set the heavy end of the taper on the floor and grasped it midway, as one might lightly hold a stout staff.

The room, lighted now by the common glow of the candles, revealed itself to be the parlor of the house elaborately decorated for the winter festival. Holly wreaths hung in the windows; the walls were garlanded; evergreen boughs were massed above the window cornices; on the white lace of window curtains many-colored autumn leaves, pressed and kept for this night, looked as though they had been blown there scatteringly by October winds. The air of the room was heavy with odors; there was summer warmth in it.

In the middle of the room stood the fir tree itself, with its top close to the ceiling and its boughs stretched toward the four walls of the room impartially - as symbolically to the four corners of the earth. It would be the only witness of all that was to take place between them: what better could there be than this messenger of silence and wild secrecy? From the mountains and valleys of the planet its race had looked out upon a million generations of men and women; and the calmness of its lot stretched across the turbulence of human passion as an ancient bridge spans a modern river.

At the apex of the Tree a star shone. Just beneath at the first forking of the boughs a candle burned. A little lower down a cross gleamed. Under the cross a white dove hung poised, its pinions outstretched as though descending out of the infinite upon some earthly object below. From many of the branches tiny bells swung. There were little horns and little trumpets. Other boughs sagged under the weight of silvery cornucopias. Native and tropical fruits were tied on here and there; and dolls were tied on also with cords around their necks, their feet dangling. There were smiling masks, like men beheaded and smiling in their death. Near the base of the Tree there was a drum. And all over the Tree from pinnacle to base glittered a tinsel like golden fleece - looking as the moss of old Southern trees seen at yellow sunset.

He stood for a while absorbed in contemplation of it. This year at his own request the decorations had been left wholly to him; now he seemed satisfied.

He turned to her eagerly.

"Do you remember what took place on Christmas Eve last year?" he asked, with a reminiscent smile. "You sat where you are sitting and I stood where I am standing. After I had finished lighting the Tree, do you remember what you said?"

After a moment she stirred and passed her fingers across her brows.

"Recall it to me," she answered. "I must have said many things. I did not know that I had said anything that would be remembered a year. Recall it to me."

"You looked at the Tree and said what a mystery it is. When and where did it begin, how and why? - this Tree that is now nourished in the affections of the human family round the world."

"Yes; I remember that."

"I resolved to find out for you. I determined to prepare during what hours I could spare from my regular college work the gratification of your wish for you as a gift from me. If I could myself find the way back through the labyrinth of ages, then I would return for you and lead you back through the story of the Christmas Tree as that story has never been seen by any one else. All this year's work, then, has been the threading of the labyrinth. Now Christmas Eve has come again, my work is finished, my gift to you is ready."

He made this announcement and stopped, leaving it to clear the air of mystery - the mystery of the secret work.

Then he resumed: "Have you, then, been the Incident in this toil as yesterday you intimated that you were? Do you now see that you have been the whole reason of it? You were excluded from any share in the work only because you could not help to prepare your own gift! That is all. What has looked like a secret in this house has been no secret. You are blinded and bewildered no longer; the hour has come when holly and cedar can speak for themselves."

Sunlight broke out all over his face.

She made no reply but said within herself:

"Ah, no! That is not the trouble. That has nothing to do with the trouble. The secret of the house is not a misunderstanding; it is life. It is not the doing of a year; it is the undoing of the years. It is not a gift to enrich me with new happiness; it is a lesson that leaves me poorer."

He went on without pausing:

"It is already late. The children interrupted us and took up part of your evening. But it is not too late for me to present to you some little part of your gift. I am going to arrange for you a short story out of the long one. The whole long story is there," he added, directing his eyes toward the manuscript at her elbow; and his voice showed how he felt a scholar's pride in it. "From you it can pass out to the world that celebrates Christmas and that often perhaps asks the same question: What is the history of the Christmas Tree? But now my story for you!"

"Wait a moment," she said, rising. She left the package where it was; and with feet that trembled against the soft carpet crossed the room and seated herself at one end of a deep sofa.

Gathering her dignity about her, she took there the posture of a listener - listening at her ease.

The sofa was of richly carved mahogany. Each end curved into a scroll like a landward wave of the sea. One of her foam-white arms rested on one of the scrolls. Her elbow, reaching beyond, touched a small table on which stood a vase of white frosted glass; over the rim of it profuse crimson carnations hung their heads. They were one of her favorite winter flowers, and he had had these sent out to her this afternoon from a hothouse of the distant town by a half-frozen messenger. Near her head curtains of crimson brocade swept down the wall to the floor from the golden-lustred window cornices. At her back were cushions of crimson silk. At the other end of the sofa her piano stood and on it lay the music she played of evenings to him, or played with thoughts of him when she was alone. And other music also which she many a time read; as Beethoven's Great Nine.

Now, along this wall of the parlor from window curtain to window curtain there stretched a festoon of evergreens and ribands put there by the children for their Christmas-Night party; and into this festoon they had fastened bunches of mistletoe, plucked from the walnut tree felled the day before - they knowing nothing, happy children!

There she reclined.

The lower outlines of her figure were lost in a rich blackness over which points of jet flashed like swarms of silvery fireflies in some too warm a night of the warm South. The blackness of her hair and the blackness of her brows contrasted with the whiteness of her bare arms and shoulders and faultless neck and faultless throat bared also. Not far away was hid the warm foam-white thigh, curved like Venus's of old out of the sea's inaccessible purity. About her wrists garlands of old family corals were clasped - the ocean's roses; and on her breast, between the night of her gown and the dawn of the flesh, coral buds flowered in beauty that could never be opened, never be rifled.

When she had crossed the room to the sofa, two aged house-dogs - setters with gentle eyes and gentle ears and gentle breeding - had followed her and lain down at her feet; and one with a thrust of his nose pushed her skirts back from the toe of her slipper and rested his chin on it.

"I will listen," she said, shrinking as yet from other speech. "I wish simply to listen. There will be time enough afterwards for what I have to say."

"Then I shall go straight through," he replied. "One minute now while I put together the story for you: it is hard to make a good short story out of so vast a one."

During these moments of waiting she saw a new picture of him. Under stress of suffering and excitement discoveries denied to calmer hours often arrive. It is as though consciousness receives a shock that causes it to yawn and open its abysses: at the bottom we see new things: sometimes creating new happiness; sometimes old happiness is taken away.

As he stood there - the man beside the Tree - into the picture entered three other men, looking down upon him from their portraits on the walls.

One portrait represented the first man of his family to scale the mountains of the Shield where its eastern rim is turned away from the reddening daybreak. Thence he had forced his way to its central portions where the skin of ever living verdure is drawn over the rocks: Anglo-Saxon, backwoodsman, borderer, great forest chief, hewing and fighting a path toward the sunset for Anglo-Saxon women and children. With his passion for the wilderness - its game, enemies, campfire and cabin, deep-lunged freedom. This ancestor had a lonely, stern, gaunt face, no modern expression in it whatsoever - the timeless face of the woods.

James Lane Allen

Near his portrait hung that of a second representative of the family. This man had looked out upon his vast parklike estates hi the central counties; and wherever his power had reached, he had used it on a great scale for the destruction of his forests. Woods-slayer, field-maker; working to bring in the period on the Shield when the hand of a man began to grasp the plough instead of the rifle, when the stallion had replaced the stag, and bellowing cattle wound fatly down into the pastures of the bison. This man had the face of his caste - the countenance of the Southern slave-holding feudal lord. Not the American face, but the Southern face of a definite era - less than national, less than modern; a face not looking far in any direction but at things close around.

From a third portrait the latest ancestor looked down. He with his contemporaries had finished the thinning of the central forest of the Shield, leaving the land as it is to-day, a rolling prairie with remnants of woodland like that crowning the hilltop near this house. This immediate forefather bore the countenance that began to develop in the Northerner and in the Southerner after the Civil War: not the Northern look nor the Southern look, but the American look - a new thing in the American face, indefinable but unmistakable.

These three men now focussed their attention upon him, the fourth of the line, standing beside the tree brought into the house. Each of them in his own way had wrought out a work for civilization, using the woods as an implement. In his own case, the woods around him having disappeared, the ancestral passion had made him a student of forestry.

The thesis upon which he took his degree was the

relation of modern forestry to modern life. A few years later in an adjunct professorship his original researches in this field began to attract attention. These had to do with the South Appalachian forest in its relation to South Appalachian civilization and thus to that of the continent.

This work had brought its reward; he was now to be drawn away from his own college and country to a Northern university.

Curiously in him there had gone on a corresponding development of an ancestral face. As the look of the wilderness hunter had changed into that of the Southern slave-holding baron, as this had changed into the modern American face unlike any other; now finally in him the national American look had broadened into something more modern still - the look of mere humanity: he did not look like an American - he looked like a man in the service of mankind.

This, which it takes thus long to recapitulate, presented itself to her as one wide vision of the truth. It left a realization of how the past had swept him along with its current; and of how the future now caught him up and bore him on, part in its problems. The old passion living on in him - forest life; a new passion born in him - human life. And by inexorable logic these two now blending themselves to-night in a story of the Christmas Tree.

But womanlike she sought to pluck out of these forces something intensely personal to which she could cling; and she did it in this wise.

In the Spring following their marriage, often after

supper they would go out on the lawn in the twilight, strolling among her flowers; she leading him this way and that way and laying upon him beautiful exactions and tyrannies: how he must do this and do that; and not do this and not do that; he receiving his orders like a grateful slave.

Then sometimes he would silently imprison her hand and lead her down the lawn and up the opposite hill to the edge of the early summer evening woods; and there on the roots of some old tree - the shadows of the forest behind them and the light of the western sky in their faces - they would stay until darkness fell, hiding their eyes from each other.

The burning horizon became a cathedral interior - the meeting of love's holiness and the Most High; the crescent dropped a silver veil upon the low green hills; wild violets were at their feet; the mosses and turf of the Shield under them. The warmth of his body was as the day's sunlight stored in the trunk of the tree; his hair was to her like its tawny bloom, native to the sun.

Life with him was enchanted madness.

He had begun. He stretched out his arm and slowly began to write on the air of the room. Sometimes in earlier years she had sat in his classroom when he was beginning a lecture; and it was thus, standing at the blackboard, that he sometimes put down the subject of his lecture for the students. Slowly now he shaped each letter and as he finished each word, he read it aloud to her:

"A STORY OF THE CHRISTMAS TREE, FOR JOSEPHINE, WIFE OF FREDERICK"

IV. THE WANDERING TALE

"Josephine!"

He uttered her name with beautiful reverence, letting the sound of it float over the Christmas Tree and die away on the garlanded walls of the room: it was his last tribute to her, a dedication.

Then he began:

"Josephine, sometimes while looking out of the study window a spring morning, I have watched you strolling among the flowers of the lawn. I have seen you linger near a honeysuckle in full bloom and question the blossoms in your questioning way - you who are always wishing to probe the heart of things, to drain out of them the red drop of their significance. But, gray-eyed querist of actuality, those fragrant trumpets could blow to your ear no message about their origin. It was where the filaments of the roots drank deepest from the mould of a dead past that you would have had to seek the true mouthpieces of their philosophy.

"So the instincts which blossom out thickly over the nature of modern man to themselves are mute. The flower exhibits itself at the tip of the vine; the instinct develops itself at the farthest outreach of life; and the point where it clamors for satisfaction is at the greatest possible distance from its birthplace. For all these instincts send their roots down through the mould of the uncivilized, down through the mould of the primitive, down into the mould of the underhuman - that ancient playhouse dedicated to low tragedies.

"While this may seem to you to be going far for a commencement of the story, it is coming near to us. The kind of man and woman we are to ourselves; the kind of husband and wife we are to each other; the kind of father and mother we are to our children; the kind of human beings we are to our fellow beings - the passions which swell as with sap the buds of those relations until they burst into their final shapes of conduct are fed from the bottom of the world's mould. You and I to-night are building the structures of our moral characters upon life-piles that sink into fathomless ooze. All we human beings dip our drinking cups into a vast delta sweeping majestically towards the sea and catch drops trickling from the springs of creation.

"It is in a vast ancestral country, a Fatherland of Old Desire, that my story lies for you and for me: drawn from the forest and from human nature as the two have worked in the destiny of the earth. I have wrested it from this Tree come out of the ancient woods into the house on this Night of the Nativity."

He made the scholar's pause and resumed, falling into the tone of easy narrative. It had already become evident that this method of telling the story would be to find what Alpine flowers he could for her amid Alpine snows.

He told her then that the oldest traceable influence in

the life of the human race is the sea. It is true that man in some ancestral form was rocked in the cradle of the deep; he rose from the waves as the islanded Greeks said of near Venus. Traces of this origin he still bears both in his body and his emotions; and together they make up his first set of memories - Sea Memories.

He deliberated a moment and then put the truth before her in a single picturesque phrase:

"Man himself is a closed living sea-shell in the chambers of which the hues of the first ocean are still fresh and its tempests still are sounding."

Next he told her how man's last marine ancestor quit one day the sea never again to return to the deep, crossed the sands of the beach and entered the forest; and how upon him, this living sea-shell, soft to impressions, the Spirit of the Forest fell to work, beginning to shape it over from sea uses to forest uses.

A thousand thousand ages the Spirit of the Forest worked at the sea-shell.

It remodelled the shell as so much clay; stood it up and twisted and branched it as young pliant oak; hammered it as forge-glowing iron; tempered it as steel; cast it as bronze; chiselled it as marble; painted it as a cloud; strung and tuned it as an instrument; lit it up as a life tower - the world's one beacon: steadily sending it onward through one trial form after another until at last had been perfected for it that angelic shape in which as man it was ever afterwards to sob and to smile.

And thus as one day a wandering sea-shell had quit the sea and entered the forest, now on another day of that infinite time there reappeared at the edge of the forest the creature it had made. On every wall of its being internal and external forest-written; and completely forest-minded: having nothing but forest knowledge, forest feeling, forest dreams, forest fancies, forest faith; so that in all it could do or know or feel or dream or imagine or believe it was forest-tethered.

At the edge of the forest then this creature uncontrollably impelled to emerge from the waving green sea of leaves as of old it had been driven to quit the rolling blue ocean of waters: Man at the dawn of our history of him.

And if the first set of race memories - Sea Memories - still endure within him, how much more powerful are the second set - the Forest Memories!

So powerful that since the dawn of history millions have perished as forest creatures only; so powerful that there are still remnant races on the globe which have never yet snapped the primitive tether and will become extinct as mere forest creatures to the last; so powerful that those highest races which have been longest out in the open - as our own Aryan race - have never ceased to be reached by the influence of the woods behind them; by the shadows of those tall morning trees falling across the mortal clearings toward the sunset.

These Master Memories, he said, filtering through the sandlike generations of our race, survive to-day as those pale attenuated affections which we call in ourselves the Love of Nature; these affections are inherited: new feelings for nature we have none. The writers of our day who speak of civilized man's love of nature as a developing sense err wholly. They are like explorers who should mistake a boundary for the interior of a continent. Man's knowledge of nature is modern, but it no more endows him with new feeling than modern knowledge of anatomy supplies him with a new bone or his latest knowledge about his blood furnishes him with an additional artery.

Old are our instincts and passions about Nature: all are Forest Memories.

But among the many-twisted mass of them there is one, he said, that contains the separate buried root of the story: Man's Forest Faith.

When the Spirit of the Forest had finished with the sea-shell, it had planted in him - there to grow forever - the root of faith that he was a forest child. His origin in the sea he had not yet discovered; the science of ages far distant in the future was to give him that. To himself forest-tethered he was also forest-born: he believed it to be his immediate ancestor, the creative father of mankind. Thus the Greeks in their oldest faith were tethered to the idea that they were descended from the plane tree; in the Sagas and Eddas the human race is tethered to the world-ash. Among every people of antiquity this forest faith sprang up and flourished: every race was tethered to some ancestral tree. In the Orient each succeeding Buddha of Indian mythology was tethered to a different tree; each god of the later classical Pantheon was similarly tethered: Jupiter to the oak, Apollo to the laurel, Bacchus to the vine, Minerva to the olive, Juno to the apple, on and on. Forest worship was universal - the most impressive and bewildering to modern science that the human spirit has ever built up. At the dawn of history began The Adoration of the Trees.

James Lane Allen

Then as man, the wanderer, walked away from his dawn across the ages toward the sunset bearing within him this root of faith, it grew with his growth. The successive growths were cut down by the successive scythes of time; but always new sprouts were put forth.

Thus to man during the earliest ages the divine dwelt as a bodily presence within the forest; but one final day the forest lost the Immortal as its indwelling creator.

Next the old forest worshipper peopled the trees with an intermediate race of sylvan deities less than divine, more than human; and long he beguiled himself with the exquisite reign and proximity of these; but the lesser could not maintain themselves in temples from which the greater had already been expelled, and they too passed out of sight down the roadway of the world.

Still the old forest faith would not let the wanderer rest; and during yet later ages he sent into the trees his own nature so that the woods became freshly endeared to him by many a story of how individuals of his own race had succeeded as tenants to the erstwhile habitations of the gods. Then this last panorama of illusion faded also, and civilized man stood face to face with the modern woods - inhabitated only by its sap and cells. The trees had drawn their bark close around them, wearing an inviolate tapestry across those portals through which so many a stranger to them had passed in and passed out; and henceforth the dubious oracle of the forest - its one reply to all man's questionings - became the Voice of its own Mystery.

After this the forest worshipper could worship the woods no more. But we must not forget that civilization as compared with the duration of human life on the planet began but yesterday: even our own Indo-European race dwells as it were on the forest edge. And the forest still reaches out and twines itself around our deepest spiritual truths: home - birth - love - prayer - death: it tries to overrun them all, to reclaim them. Thus when we build our houses, instinctively we attempt by some clump of trees to hide them and to shelter ourselves once more inside the forest; in some countries whenever a child is born, a tree is planted as its guardian in nature; in our marriage customs the forest still riots as master of ceremonies with garlands and fruits; our prayers strike against the forest shaped hi cathedral stone - memory of the grove, God's first temple; and when we die, it is the tree that is planted beside us as the sentinel of our rest. Even to this day the sight of a treeless grave arouses some obscure instinct in us that it is God-forsaken.

Yes, he said, whatsoever modern temple man has anywhere reared for his spirit, over the walls of it have been found growing the same leaf and tendril: he has introduced the tree into the ritual of every later world-worship; and thus he has introduced the evergreen into the ritual of Christianity.

This then is the meaning of the Christmas Tree and of its presence at the Nativity. At the dawn of history we behold man worshipping the tree as the Creator literally present on the earth; in our time we see him using that tree in the worship of the creative Father's Son come to earth in the Father's stead.

"On this evergreen in the room falls the radiance of these brief tapers of the night; but on it rests also the long light of that spiritual dawn when man began his Adoration of the Trees. It is the forest taking its place once more beside the long-lost Immortal."

Here he finished the first part of his story. That he should address her thus and that she thus should listen had in it nothing unusual for them. For years it had been his wont to traverse with her the ground of his lectures, and she shared his thought before it reached others. It was their high and equal comradeship. Wherever his mind could go hers went - a brilliant torch, a warming sympathy.

But to-night his words had fallen on her as withered leaves on a motionless figure of stone. If he was sensible of this change in her, he gave no sign. And after a moment he passed to the remaining part of the story.

"Thus far I have been speaking to you of the bare tree in wild nature: here it is loaded with decorations; and now I want to show you that they too are Forest Memories - that since the evergreen moved over into the service of Christianity, one by one like a flock of birds these Forest Memories have followed it and have alighted amid its branches. Everything here has its story. I am going to tell you in each case what that story is; I am going to interpret everything on the Christmas Tree and the other Christmas decorations in the room."

It was at this point that her keen attention became fixed on him and never afterwards wavered. If everything had its story, the mistletoe would have its; he must interpret that: and thus he himself unexpectedly had brought about the situation she wished. She would meet him at that symbolic bough: there be rendered the Judgment of the Years! And now as one sits down at some point of a road where a traveller must arrive, she waited for him there.

He turned to the Tree and explained briefly that as soon as the forest worshipper began the worship of the tree, he began to bring to it his offerings and to hang these on the boughs; for religion consists in offering something: to worship is to give. In after ages when man had learned to build shrines and temples, he still kept up his primitive custom of bringing to the altar his gifts and sacrifices; but during that immeasurable time before he had learned to carve wood or to set one stone on another, he was bringing his offerings to the grove - the only cathedral he had. And this to him was not decoration; it was prayer. So that in our age of the world when we playfully decorate the Christmas Tree it is a survival of grave rites in the worship of primitive man and is as ancient as forest worship itself.

And now he began.

With the pointer in his hand he touched the star at the apex of the fir. This, he said, was commonly understood to represent the Star of Bethlehem which guided the wise men of the East to the manger on the Night of the Nativity - the Star of the New Born. But modern discoveries show that the records of ancient Chaldea go back four or five thousand years before the Christian era; and as far back as they have been traced, we find the wise men of the East worshipping this same star and being guided by it in their spiritual wanderings as they searched for the incarnation of the Divine. They worshipped it as the star of peace and goodness and purity. Many a pious Wolfram in those dim centuries no doubt sang his evening hymn to the same star, for love of some Chaldean Elizabeth - both he and she blown about the desert how many centuries now as dust. Moreover on these records the star and the Tree are brought together as here side by side. And the story of the star leads backward to one of the first things that man ever worshipped as he looked beyond the forest: the light of the heavens floating in the depth of space - light that he wanted but could not grasp.

He touched the next object on the Tree - the candle under the star - and went on:

Imagine, he said, the forest worshipper as at the end of ages having caught this light - having brought it down in the language of his myth from heaven to earth: that is, imagine the star in space as having become a star in his hand - the candle: the star worshipper had now become also the fire worshipper. Thus the candle leads us back to the fire worshippers of ancient Persia - those highlands of the spirit seeking light. We think of the Christmas candle on the Tree as merely borrowed from the candle of the altar for the purpose of illumination; but the use of it goes back to a time when the forest worshipper, now also the fire worshipper, hung his lights on the trees, having no other altar. Far down toward modern times the temples of the old Prussians, for example, were oak groves, and among them a hierarchy of priests was ordained to keep the sacred fire perpetually burning at the root of the sacred oak.

He touched the third object on the tree - the cross under the candle - and went on:

"To the Christian believer the cross signifies one supreme event: Calvary and the tragedy of the Crucifixion. It was what the Marys saw and the apostles that morning in Gethsemane. But no one in that age thought of the cross as a Christian symbol. John and Peter and Paul and the rest went down into their graves without so regarding it. The Magdalene never clung to it with life-tired arms, nor poured out at the foot of it the benizon of her tears. Not until the third century after Christ did the Bishops assembled at Nice announce it a Christian symbol. But it was a sacred emblem in the dateless antiquity of Egypt. To primitive man it stood for that sacred light and fire of life which was himself. For he himself is a cross - the first cross he has ever known. The faithful may truly think of the Son of Man as crucified as the image of humanity. And thus ages before Christ, cross worship and forest worship were brought together: for instance, among the Druids who hunted for an oak, two boughs of which made with the trunk of the tree the figure of the cross; and on these three they cut the names of three of their gods and this was holy-cross wood."

He moved the pointer down until he touched the fourth object on the tree - the dove under the cross, and went on:

"In the mind of the Christian believer this represents the white dove of the New Testament which descended on the Son of Man when the heavens were opened. So in Parsifal the white dove descends, overshadowing the Grail. But ages before Christ the prolific white dove of Syria was worshipped throughout the Orient as the symbol of reproductive Nature: and to this day the Almighty is there believed to manifest himself under this form. In ancient Mesopotamia the divine mother of nature is often represented with this dove as having actually alighted on her shoulder or in her open hand. And here again forest worship early became associated with the worship of the dove; for, sixteen hundred years before Christ, we find the dove nurtured in the oak grove at Dodona where its presence was an augury and its wings an omen."

On he went, touching one thing after another, tracing the story of each backward till it was lost in antiquity and showing how each was entwined with forest worship.

He touched the musical instruments; the bell, the drum. The bell, he said, was used in Greece by the Priests of Bacchus in the worship of the vine. And vine worship was forest worship. Moreover, in the same oak grove at Dodona bells were tied to the oak boughs and their tinklings also were sacred auguries. The drum, which the modern boy beats on Christmas Day, was beaten ages before Christ in the worship of Confucius: the story of it dies away toward what was man's first written music in forgotten China. In the first century of the Christian era, on one of the most splendid of the old Buddhist sculptures, boys are represented as beating the drum in the worship of the sacred tree - once more showing how music passed into the service of forest faith.

He touched the cornucopia; and he traced its story back to the ram's horn - the primitive cup of libation, used for a drinking cup and used also to pour out the last product of the vine in honor of the vine itself - the forest's first goblet.

He touched the fruits and the flowers on the Tree: these were oldest of all, perhaps, he said; for before the forest worshipper had learned to shape or fabricate any offerings of his own skill, he could at least bring to the divine tree and hang on it the flower of spring, the wild fruit of autumn.

He kept on until only three things on the Tree were left uninterpreted; the tinsel, the masks, and the dolls. He told her that he had left these to the last for a reason: seemingly they were the most trivial but really the most grave; for by means of them most clearly could be traced the presence of great law running through the progress of humanity.

He drew her attention to the tinsel that covered the tree, draping it like a yellow moss. It was of no value, he said, but in the course of ages it had taken the place of the offering of actual gold in forest worship: a once universal custom of adorning the tree with everything most precious to the giver in token of his sacrifice and self-sacrifice. Even in Jeremiah is an account of the lading of the sacred tree with gold and ornaments. Herodotus relates that when Xerxes was invading Lydia, on the march he saw a divine tree and had it honored with golden robes and gifts. Livy narrates that when Romulus slew his enemy on the site of the Eternal City, he hung rich spoils on the oak of the Capitoline Hill. And this custom of decorating the tree with actual gold goes back in history until we can meet it coming down to us in the story of Jason and the Golden Fleece and in that of the Golden Apples of the Hesperides. Now the custom has dwindled to this tinsel flung over the Christmas Tree - the mock sacrifice for the real.

He touched the masks and unfolded the grim story that lay behind their mockery. It led back to the common custom in antiquity of sacrificing prisoners of war or condemned criminals or innocent victims in forest worship and of hanging their heads on the branches:

James Lane Allen

we know this to have been the practice among Gallic and Teuton tribes. In the course of time, when such barbarity could be tolerated no longer, the mock countenance replaced the real.

He touched the dolls and revealed their sad story. Like the others, its long path led to antiquity and to the custom of sacrificing children in forest worship. How common this custom was the early literature of the human race too abundantly testifies. We encounter the trace of it in Abraham's sacrifice of Isaac - arrested by the command of Jehovah. But Abraham would never have thought of slaying his son to propitiate his God, had not the custom been well established. In the case of Jephthah's daughter the sacrifice was actually allowed. We come upon the same custom in the fate of Iphigenia - at a critical turning point in the world's mercy; in her stead the life of a lesser animal, as in Isaac's case, was accepted. When the protective charity of mankind turned against the inhumanity of the old faiths, then the substitution of the mock for the real sacrifice became complete. And now on the boughs of the Christmas Tree where richly we come upon vestiges of primitive rites only these playful toys are left to suggest the massacre of the innocent.

He had covered the ground; everything had yielded its story. All the little stories, like pathways running backward into the distance and ever converging, met somewhere in lost ages; they met in forest worship and they met in some sacrifice by the human heart.

And thus he drew his conclusion as the lesson of the night:

"Thus, Josephine, my story ends for you and for me.

The Christmas Tree is all that is left of a forest memory. The forest worshipper could not worship without giving, because to worship is to give: therefore he brought his gifts to the forest - his first altar. These gifts, remember, were never, as with us, decorations. They were his sacrifices and self-sacrifices. In all the religions he has had since, the same law lives. In his lower religions he has sacrificed the better to the worse; in the higher ones he has sacrificed the worst to the best. If the race should ever outgrow all religion whatsoever, it would still have to worship what is highest in human nature and so worshipping, it would still be ruled by the ancient law of sacrifice become the law of self-sacrifice: it would still be necessary to offer up what is low in us to what is higher. Only one portion of mankind has ever believed in Jerusalem; but every religion has known its own Calvary."

He turned away from the Tree toward her and awaited her appreciation. She had sat watching him without a movement and without a word. But when at last she asked him a question, she spoke as a listener who wakens from a long revery.

"Have you finished the story for me?" she inquired.

"I have finished the story for you," he replied without betraying disappointment at her icy reception of it.

Keeping her posture, she raised one of her white arms above her head, turning her face up also until the swanlike curve of the white throat showed; and with quivering finger tips she touched some sprays of mistletoe pendent from the garland on the wall:

"You have not interpreted this," she said, her mind

fixed on that sole omission.

"I have not explained that," he admitted.

She sat up, and for the first time looked with intense interest toward the manuscript on the table across the room.

"Have you explained it there?"

"I have not explained it there."

"But why?" she said with disappointment.

"I did not wish you to read that story, Josephine."

"But why, Frederick?" she inquired, startled into wonderment.

He smiled: "If I told you why, I might as well tell you the story."

"But why do you not wish to tell me the story?"

He answered with warning frankness: "If you once saw it as a picture, the picture would be coming back to you at times the rest of your life darkly."

She protested: "If it is dark to you, why should I not share the darkness of it? Have we not always looked at life's shadows together? And thus seeing life, have not bright things been doubly bright to us and dark things but half as dark?"

He merely repeated his warning: "It is a story of a crueler age than ours. It goes back to the forest worship of the Druids."

She answered: "So long as our own age is cruel, what room is left to take seriously the mere stories of crueler ones? Am I to shrink from the forest worship of the Druids? Is there any story of theirs not printed in books? Are not the books in libraries? Are they not put in libraries to be read? If others read them, may not I? And since when must I begin to dread anything in books? Or anything in life? And since when did we begin to look at life apart, we who have always looked at it with four eyes?"

"I have always told you there are things to see with four eyes, things to see with two, and things to see with none."

With sudden intensity her white arm went up again and touched the mistletoe.

"Tell me the story of this!" she pleaded as though she demanded a right. As she spoke, her thumb and fore-finger meeting on a spray, they closed and went through it like a pair of shears; and a bunch of the white pearls of the forest dropped on the ridge of her shoulder and were broken apart and rolled across her breast into her lap.

He looked grave; silence or speech - which were better for her? Either, he now saw, would give her pain.

"Happily the story is far away from us," he said, as though he were half inclined to grant her request.

"If it is far away, bring it near! Bring it into the room as you brought the stories of the star and the candle and the cross and the dove and the others! Make it live before my eyes! Enact it before me! Steep me in it as you have steeped yourself!"

He held back a long time: "You who are so safe in good, why know evil?"

"Frederick," she cried, "I shall have to insist upon your telling me this story. And if you should keep any part of it back, I would know. Then tell it all: if it is dark, let each shadow have its shade; give each heavy part its heaviness; let cruelty be cruelty - and truth be truth!"

He stood gazing across the centuries, and when he began, there was a change in him; something personal was beginning to intrude itself into the narrative of the historian:

"Imagine the world of our human nature in the last centuries before Palestine became Holy Land. Athens stood with her marbles glistening by the blue Ægean, and Greek girls with fillets and sandals - the living images of those pale sculptured shapes that are the mournful eternity of Art - Greek girls were being chosen for the secret rites in the temple at Ephesus. The sun of Italy had not yet browned the little children who were to become the brown fathers and mothers of the brown soldiers of Cæsar's legions; and twenty miles south of Rome, in the sacred grove of Dodona, - where the motions of oak boughs were auguries, and the flappings of the wings of white doves were divine messages, and the tinkling of bells in the foliage had divine meanings, - in this grove the virgins of Latium, as the Greek girls of Ephesus, were once a year appointed to undergo similar rites. To the south

Pompeii, with its night laughter and song sounding far out toward the softly lapping Mediterranean and up the slopes of its dread volcano, drained its goblet and did not care, emptied it as often as filled and asked for nothing more. A little distance off Herculaneum, with its tender dreams of Greece but with its arms around the breathing image of Italy, slept - uncovered.

"Beyond Italy to the north, on the other side of the eternal snowcaps, lay unknown Gaul, not yet dreaming of the Cæsar who was to conquer it; and across the wild sea opposite Gaul lay the wooded isle of Britain. All over that island one forest; in that forest one worship; in that worship one tree - the oak of England; and on that oak one bough - the mistletoe."

He spoke to her awhile about the oak, describing the place it had in the early civilizations of the human race. In the Old Testament it was the tree of the Hebrew idols and of Jehovah. In Greece it was the tree of Zeus, the most august and the most human of the gods. In Italy it was the tree of Jove, great father of immortals and of mankind. After the gods passed, it became the tree of the imperial Cæsars. After the Cæsars had passed, it was the oak that Michael Angelo in the Middle Ages scattered over the ceiling of the Sistine Chapel near the creation of man and his expulsion from Paradise - there as always the chosen tree of human desire. In Britain it was the sacred tree of Druidism: there the Arch Druid and his fellow-priests performed none of their rites without using its leaves and branches: never anywhere in the world was the oak worshipped with such ceremonies and sacrifices as there.

Imagine then a scene - the chief Nature Festival of that

forest worship: the New Year's day of the Druids.

A vast concourse of people, men and women and children, are on their way to the forest; they are moving toward an oak tree that has been found with mistletoe growing on it - growing there so seldom. As the excited throng come in sight of it, they hail it with loud cries of reverence and delight. Under it they gather; there a banquet is spread. In the midst of the assemblage one figure towers - the Arch Druid. Every eye is fixed fearfully on him, for on whomsoever his own eye may fall with wrath, he may be doomed to become one of the victims annually sacrificed to the oak.

A gold chain is around his neck; gold bands are around his arms. He is clad in robes of spotless white. He ascends the tree to a low bough, and making a hollow in the folds of his robes, he crops with a golden pruning hook the mistletoe and so catches it as it falls. Then it is blessed and scattered among the throng, and the priest prays that each one so receiving it may receive also the divine favor and blessing of which it is Nature's emblem. Two white bulls, the horns of which have never hitherto been touched, are now adorned with fillets and are slaughtered in sacrifice.

Then at last it is over, the people are gone, the forest is left to itself, and the New Year's ceremony of cutting the mistletoe from the oak is at an end.

Here he ended the story.

She had sat leaning far forward, her fingers interlocked and her brows knitted. When he stopped, she sat up and studied him a moment in bewilderment:

"But why did you call that a dark story?" she asked. "Where is the cruelty? It is beautiful, and I shall never forget it and it will never throw a dark image on my mind: New Year's day - the winter woods - the journeying throng - the oak - the bough - the banquet beneath - the white bulls with fillets on their horns - the white-robed priest - the golden sickle in his hand - the stroke that severs the mistletoe - the prayer that each soul receiving any smallest piece will be blessed in life's sorrows! If I were a great painter, I should like to paint that scene. In the centre should be some young girl, pressing to her heart what she believed to be heaven's covenant with her under the guise of a blossom. How could you have wished to withhold such a story from me?"

He smiled at her a little sadly.

"I have not yet told you all," he said, "but I have told you enough."

Instantly she bent far over toward him with intuitive scrutiny. Under her breath one word escaped:

"Ah!"

It was the breath of a discovery - a discovery of something unknown to her.

"I am sparing you, Josephine!"

She stretched each arm along the back of the sofa and pinioned the wood in her clutch.

"Are you sparing me?" she asked in a tone of torture. "Or are you sparing yourself?"

The heavy staff on which he stood leaning dropped from his relaxed grasp to the floor. He looked down at it a moment and then calmly picked it up.

"I am going to tell you the story," he said with a new quietness.

She was aroused by some change in him.

"I will not listen! I do not wish to hear it!"

"You will have to listen," he said. "It is better for you to know. Better for any human being to know any truth than suffer the bane of wrong thinking. When you are free to judge, it will be impossible for you to misjudge."

"I have not misjudged you! I have not judged you! In some way that I do not understand you are judging yourself!"

He stepped back a pace - farther away from her - and he drew himself up. In the movement there was instinctive resentment. And the right not to be pried into - not even by the nearest.

The step which had removed him farther from her had brought him nearer to the Christmas Tree at his back. A long, three-fingered bough being thus pressed against was forced upward and reappeared on one of his shoulders. The movement seemed human: it was like the conscious hand of the tree. The fir, standing there decked out in the artificial tawdriness of a double-dealing race, laid its wild sincere touch on him - as sincere as the touch of dying human fingers - and let its passing youth flow into him. It attracted his attention, and he turned his head toward it as with recognition. Other boughs near the floor likewise thrust themselves forward, hiding his feet so that he stood ankle-deep in forestry.

This reunion did not escape her. Her overwrought imagination made of it a sinister omen: the bough on his shoulder rested there as the old forest claim; the boughs about his feet were the ancestral forest tether. As he had stepped backward from her, Nature had asserted the earlier right to him. In strange sickness and desolation of heart she waited.

He stood facing her but looking past her at centuries long gone; the first sound of his voice registered upon her ear some message of doom:

"Listen, Josephine!"

She buried her face in her hands.

"I cannot! I will not!"

"You will have to listen. You know that for some years, apart from my other work, I have been gathering together the woodland customs of our people and trying to trace them back to their origin and first meaning. In our age of the world we come upon many playful forest survivals of what were once grave things. Often in our play and pastimes and lingering superstitions about the forest we cross faint traces of what were once vital realities.

"Among these there has always been one that until recently I have never understood. Among country people oftenest, but heard of everywhere, is the saying that if a girl is caught standing under the mistletoe, she may be kissed by the man who thus finds her. I have always thought that this ceremony and playful sacrifice led back to some ancient rite - I could not discover what. Now I know."

In a voice full of a new delicacy and scarcely audible, he told her.

It is another scene in the forest of Britain. This time it is not the first day of the year - the New Year's day of the Druids when they celebrated the national festival of the oak. But it is early summer, perhaps the middle of May - May in England - with the young beauty of the woods. It is some hushed evening at twilight. The new moon is just silvering the tender leaves and creating a faint shadow under the trees. The hawthorn is in bloom - red and white - and not far from the spot, hidden in some fragrant tuft of this, a nightingale is singing, singing, singing.

Lifting itself above the smaller growths stands the young manhood of the woods - a splendid oak past its thirtieth year, representing its youth and its prime conjoined. In its trunk is the summer heat of the all-day sun. Around its roots is velvet turf, and there are wild violet beds. Its huge arms are stretched toward the ground as though reaching for some object they would clasp; and on one of these arms as its badge of divine authority, worn there as a knight might wear the colors of his Sovereign, grows the mistletoe. There he stands - the Forest Lover.

The woods wait, the shadows deepen, the hush is more intense, the moon's rays begin to be golden, the song of the nightingale grows more passionate, the beds of moss and violets wait.

Then the shrubbery is tremblingly parted at some place and upon the scene a young girl enters - her hair hanging down - her limbs most lightly clad - the flush of red hawthorn on the white hawthorn of her skin - in her eyes love's great need and mystery. Step by step she comes forward, her fingers trailing against whatsoever budding wayside thing may stay her strength. She draws nearer to the oak, searching amid its boughs for that emblem which she so dreads to find and yet more dreads not to find: the emblem of a woman's fruitfulness which the young oak - the Forest Lover - reaches down toward her. Finding it, beneath it with one deep breath of surrender she takes her place – the virgin's tryst with the tree - there to be tested.

Such is the command of the Arch Druid: it is obedience - submission to that test - or death for her as a sacrifice to the oak which she has rejected.

Again the shrubbery is parted, rudely pushed aside, and a man enters - a tried and seasoned man - a human oak - counterpart of the Forest Lover - to officiate at the test.

*   *   *   *   *

He was standing there in the parlor of his house and in the presence of his wife. But in fealty he was gone: he was in the summer woods of ancestral wandering, the fatherland of Old Desire.

He was the man treading down the shrubbery; it was *his* feet that started toward the oak; *his* eye that searched for the figure half fainting under the bough;

James Lane Allen

for *him* the bed of moss and violets - the hair falling over the eyes - the loosened girdle - the breasts of hawthorn white and pink - the listening song of the nightingale - the silence of the summer woods - the seclusion - the full surrender of the two under that bough of the divine command, to escape the penalty of their own death.

The blaze of uncontrollable desire was all over him; the fire of his own story had treacherously licked him like a wind-bent flame. The light that she had not seen in his eyes for so long rose in them - the old, unfathomable, infolding tenderness. A quiver ran around his tense nostrils.

And now one little phrase which he had uttered so sacredly years before and had long since forgotten rose a second time to his lips - tossed there by a second tide of feeling. On the silence of the room fell his words:

"Bride of the Mistletoe!"

The storm that had broken over him died away. He shut his eyes on the vanishing scene: he opened them upon her.

He had told her the truth about the story; he may have been aware or he may not have been aware that he had revealed to her the truth about himself.

"This is what I would have kept from you, Josephine," he said quietly.

She was sitting there before him - the mother of his children, of the sleeping ones, of the buried ones - the butterfly broken on the wheel of years: lustreless and useless now in its summer.

She sat there with the whiteness of death.

James Lane Allen

V. THE ROOM OF THE SILENCES

The Christmas candles looked at her flickeringly; the little white candles of purity, the little red candles of love. The holly in the room concealed its bold gay berries behind its thorns, and the cedar from the faithful tree beside the house wall had need now of its bitter rosary.

Her first act was to pay what is the first debt of a fine spirit - the debt of courtesy and gratitude.

"It is a wonderful story, Frederick," she said in a manner which showed him that she referred to the beginning of his story and not to the end.

"As usual you have gone your own way about it, opening your own path into the unknown, seeing what no one else has seen, and bringing back what no one else ever brought. It is a great revelation of things that I never dreamed of and could never have imagined. I appreciate your having done this for me; it has taken time and work, but it is too much for me to-night. It is too new and too vast. I must hereafter try to understand it. And there will be leisure enough. Nor can it lose by waiting. But now there is something that cannot wait, and I wish to speak to you about that; Frederick, I am going to ask you some questions about the last part of the story. I have been wanting to ask you a long time:

the story gives me the chance and - the right."

He advanced a step toward her, disengaging himself from the evergreen.

"I will answer them," he said. "If they can be answered."

And thus she sat and thus he stood as the questions and answers passed to and fro. They were solemn questions and solemn replies, drawn out of the deeps of life and sinking back into them.

"Frederick," she said, "for many years we have been happy together, so happy! Every tragedy of nature has stood at a distance from us except the loss of our children. We have lived on a sunny pinnacle of our years, lifted above life's storms. But of course I have realized that sooner or later our lot must become the common one: if we did not go down to Sorrow, Sorrow would climb to us; and I knew that on the heights it dwells best. That is why I wish to say to you to-night what I shall: I think fate's hour has struck for me; I am ready to hear it. Its arrow has already left the bow and is on its way; I open my heart to receive it. This is as I have always wished; I have said that if life had any greatest tragedy, for me, I hoped it would come when I was happiest; thus I should confront it all. I have never drunk half of my cup of happiness, as you know, and let the other half waste; I must go equally to the depth of any suffering. Worse than the suffering, I think, would be the feeling that I had shirked some of it, had stepped aside, or shut my eyes, or in any manner shown myself a cowardly soul."

After a pause she went over this subject as though she

James Lane Allen

were not satisfied that she had made it clear.

"I have always said that the real pathos of things is the grief that comes to us in life when life is at its best - when no one is to blame - when no one has committed a fault - when suffering is meted out to us as the reward of our perfect obedience to the laws of nature. In earlier years when we used to read Keats together, who most of all of the world's poets felt the things that pass, even then I was wondering at the way in which he brings this out: that to understand Sorrow it must be separated from sorrows: they would be like shadows darkening the bright disk of life's clear tragedy, thus rendering it less bravely seen.

"And so he is always telling us not to summon sad pictures nor play with mournful emblems; not to feign ourselves as standing on the banks of Lethe, gloomiest of rivers; nor to gather wolf's bane and twist the poison out of its tight roots; nor set before us the cup of hemlock; nor bind about our temples the ruby grape of nightshade; nor count over the berries of the yew tree which guards sad places; nor think of the beetle ticking in the bed post, nor watch the wings of the death moth, nor listen to the elegy of the owl - the voice of ruins. Not these! they are the emblems of our sorrows. But the emblems of Sorrow are beautiful things at their perfect moment; a red peony just opening, a rainbow seen for an instant on the white foam, youth not yet faded but already fading, joy with its finger on his lips, bidding adieu.

"And so with all my happiness about me, I wish to know life's tragedy. And to know it, Frederick, not to infer it: *I want to be told.*"

"If you can be told, you shall be told," he said.

She changed her position as though seeking physical relief and composure. Then she began:

"Years ago when you were a student in Germany, you had a college friend. You went home with him two or three years at Christmas and celebrated the German Christmas. It was in this way that we came to have the Christmas Tree in our house - through memory of him and of those years. You have often described to me how you and he in summer went Alpine climbing, and far up in some green valley girdled with glaciers lay of afternoons under some fir tree, reading and drowsing in the crystalline air. You told me of your nights of wandering down the Rhine together when the heart turns so intimately to the heart beside it. He was German youth and song and dream and happiness to you. Tell me this: before you lost him that last summer over the crevasse, had you begun to tire of him? Was there anything in you that began to draw back from anything in him? As you now look back at the friendship of your youth, have the years lessened your regret for him?"

He answered out of the ideals of his youth:

"The longer I knew him, the more I loved him. I never tired of being with him. Nothing in me ever drew back from anything in him. When he was lost, the whole world lost some of its strength and nobility. After all the years, if he could come back, he would find me unchanged - that friend of my youth!"

With a peculiar change of voice she asked next:

"The doctor, Herbert and Elsie's father, our nearest neighbor, your closest friend now in middle life. You see a great deal of the doctor; he is often here, and you and he often sit up late at night, talking with one another about many things: do you ever tire of the doctor and wish him away? Have you any feeling toward him that you try to keep secret from me? Can you be a perfectly frank man with this friend of your middle life?"

"The longer I know him the more I like him, honor him, trust him. I never tire of his companionship or his conversation; I have no disguises with him and need none."

"The children! As the children grow older do you care less for them? Do they begin to wear on you? Are they a clog, an interference? Have Harold and Elizabeth ceased forming new growths of affection in you? Do you ever unconsciously seek pretexts for avoiding them?"

"The older they grow, the more I love them. The more they interest me and tempt away from work and duties. I am more drawn to be with them and I live more and more in the thought of what they are becoming."

"Your work! Does your work attract you less than formerly? Does it develop in you the purpose to be something more or stifle in you the regret to be something less? Is it a snare to idleness or a goad to toil?"

"As the mariner steers for the lighthouse, as the hound runs down the stag, as the soldier wakes to the bugle, as the miner digs for fortune, as the drunkard drains the cup, as the saint watches the cross, I follow my work, I follow my work."

"Life, life itself, does it increase in value or lessen? Is the world still morning to you with your work ahead or afternoon when you begin to tire and to think of rest?"

"The world to me is as early morning to a man going forth to his work. Where the human race is from and whither it is hurrying and why it exists at all; why a human being loves what it loves and hates what it hates; why it is faithful when it could be unfaithful and faithless when it should be true; how civilized man can fight single handed against the ages that were his lower past - how he can develop self-renunciation out of selfishness and his own wisdom out of surrounding folly, - all these are questions that mean more and more. My work is but beginning and the world is morning."

"This house! Are you tired of it now that it is older? Would you rather move into a new one?"

"I love this house more and more. No other dwelling could take its place. Any other could be but a shelter; this is home. And I care more for it now that the signs of age begin to settle on it. If it were a ruin, I should love it best!"

She leaned over and looked down at the two setters lying at her feet.

"Do you care less for the dogs of the house as they grow older?"

"I think more of them and take better care of them now

James Lane Allen

that their hunting days are over."

"The friend of your youth - the friend of your middle age - the children - your profession - the world of human life - this house - the dogs of the house - you care more for them all as time passes?"

"I care more for them all as time passes."

Then there came a great stillness in the room - the stillness of all listening years.

"Am I the only thing that you care less for as time passes?"

There was no reply.

"Am I in the way?"

There was no reply.

"Would you like to go over it all again with another?"

There was no reply.

She had hidden her face in her hands and pressed her head against the end of the sofa. Her whole figure shrank lower, as though to escape being touched by him - to escape the blow of his words. No words came. There was no touch.

A moment later she felt that he must be standing over her, looking down at her. She would respond to his hand on the back of her neck. He must be kneeling beside her; his arms would infold her. Then with a kind of incredible terror she realized that he was not there.

At first she could so little believe it, that with her face still buried in one hand she searched the air for him with the other, expecting to touch him.

Then she cried out to him:

"Isn't there anything you can say to me?"

Silence lasted.

"*Oh, Fred! Fred! Fred! Fred*!"

In the stillness she began to hear something - the sound of his footsteps moving on the carpet. She sat up.

The room was getting darker; he was putting out the candles. It was too dark already to see his face. With fascination she began to watch his hand. How steady it was as it moved among the boughs, extinguishing the lights. Out they went one by one and back into their darkness returned the emblems of darker ages - the Forest Memories.

A solitary taper was left burning at the pinnacle of the Tree under the cross: that highest torch of love shining on everything that had disappeared.

He quietly put it out.

Yet the light seemed not put out, but instantly to have travelled through the open parlor door into the adjoining room, her bedroom; for out of that there now streamed a suffused red light; it came from the lamp near the great bed in the shadowy corner.

This lamp poured its light through a lampshade having

the semblance of a bursting crimson peony as some morning in June the flower with the weight of its own splendor falls face downward on the grass. And in that room this soft lamp-light fell here and there on crimson winter draperies. He had been living alone as a bachelor before he married her. After they became engaged he, having watched for some favorite color of hers, had had this room redecorated in that shade. Every winter since she had renewed in this way or that way these hangings, and now the bridal draperies remained unchanged - after the changing years.

He replaced the taper against the wall and came over and stood before her, holding out his hands to help her rise.

She arose without his aid and passed around him, moving toward her bedroom. With arms outstretched guarding her but not touching her, he followed close, for she was unsteady. She entered her bedroom and crossed to the door of his bedroom; she pushed this open, and keeping her face bent aside waited for him to go in. He went in and she closed the door on him and turned the key. Then with a low note, with which the soul tears out of itself something that has been its life, she made a circlet of her white arms against the door and laid her profile within this circlet and stood - the figure of Memory.

Thus sometimes a stranger sees a marble figure standing outside a tomb where some story of love and youth ended: some stranger in a far land, - walking some afternoon in those quieter grounds where all human stories end; an autumn bird in the bare branches fluting of its mortality and his heart singing with the bird of one lost to him - lost to him in his own country.

On the other side of the door the silence was that of a tomb. She had felt confident - so far as she had expected anything - that he would speak to her through the door, try to open it, plead with her to open it. Nothing of the kind occurred.

Why did he not come back? What bolt could have separated her from him?

The silence began to weigh upon her.

Then in the tense stillness she heard him moving quietly about, getting ready for bed. There were the same movements, familiar to her for years. She would not open the door, she could not leave it, she could not stand, no support was near, and she sank to the floor and sat there, leaning her brow against the lintel.

On the other side the quiet preparations went on.

She heard him take off his coat and vest and hang them on the back of a chair. The buttons made a little scraping sound against the wood. Then he went to his dresser and took off his collar and tie, and he opened a drawer and laid out a night-shirt. She heard the creaking of a chair under him as he threw one foot and then the other up across his knee and took off his shoes and socks. Then there reached her the soft movements of his bare feet on the carpet (despite her agony the old impulse started in her to caution him about his slippers). Then followed the brushing of his teeth and the deliberate bathing of his hands. Then was audible the puff of breath with which he blew out his lamp after he had turned it low; and then, - on the other side of the door, - just above her ear his knock sounded.

James Lane Allen

The same knock waited for and responded to throughout the years; so often with his little variations of playfulness. Many a time in early summer when out-of-doors she would be reminded of it by hearing some bird sounding its love signal on a piece of dry wood - that tap of heart-beat. Now it crashed close to her ear.

Such strength came back to her that she rose as lightly as though her flesh were but will and spirit. When he knocked again, she was across the room, sitting on the edge of her bed with her palms pressed together and thrust between her knees: the instinctive act of a human animal suddenly chilled to the bone.

The knocking sounded again.

"Was there anything you needed?" she asked fearfully.

There was no response but another knock.

She hurriedly raised her voice to make sure that it would reach him.

"Was there anything you wanted?"

As no response came, the protective maternal instinct took greater alarm, and she crossed to the door of his room and she repeated her one question:

"Did you forget anything?"

Her mind refused to release itself from the iteration of that idea: it was some *thing* - not herself - that he wanted.

He knocked.

Her imagination, long oppressed by his silence, now made of his knock some signal of distress. It took on the authority of an appeal not to be denied. She unlocked the door and opened it a little way, and once more she asked her one poor question.

His answer to it came in the form of a gentle pressure against the door, breaking down her resistance. As she applied more strength, this was as gently overcome; and when the opening was sufficient, he walked past her into the room.

How hushed the house! How still the world outside as the cloud wove in darkness its mantle of light!

VI. THE WHITE DAWN

Day was breaking.

The crimson curtains of the bedroom were drawn close, but from behind their outer edges faint flanges of light began to advance along the wall. It was a clear light reflected from snow which had sifted in against the window-panes, was banked on the sills outside, ridged the yard fence, peaked the little gate-posts, and buried the shrubbery. There was no need to look out in order to know that it had stopped snowing, that the air was windless, and that the stars were flashing silver-pale except one - great golden-croziered shepherd of the thick, soft-footed, moving host.

It was Christmas morning on the effulgent Shield.

Already there was sufficient light in the room to reveal - less as actual things than as brown shadows of the memory - a gay company of socks and stockings hanging from the mantelpiece; sufficient to give outline to the bulk of a man asleep on the edge of the bed; and it exposed to view in a corner of the room farthest from the rays a woman sitting in a straight-backed chair, a shawl thrown about her shoulders over her night-dress.

He always slept till he was awakened; the children,

having stayed up past their usual bedtime, would sleep late also; she had the white dawn to herself in quietness.

She needed it.

Sleep could not have come to her had she wished. She had not slept and she had not lain down, and the sole endeavor during those shattered hours had been to prepare herself for his awakening. She was not yet ready - she felt that during the rest of her life she should never be quite ready to meet him again. Scant time remained now.

Soon all over the Shield indoor merriment and outdoor noises would begin. Wherever in the lowlands any many-chimneyed city, proud of its size, rose by the sweep of watercourses, or any little inland town was proud of its smallness and of streets that terminated in the fields; whereever any hamlet marked the point at which two country roads this morning made the sign of the white cross, or homesteads stood proudly castled on woody hilltops, or warmed the heart of the beholder from amid their olive-dark winter pastures; or far away on the shaggy uplift of the Shield wherever any cabin clung like a swallow's nest against the gray Appalachian wall - everywhere soon would begin the healthy outbreak of joy among men and women and children - glad about themselves, glad in one another, glad of human life in a happy world. The many-voiced roar and din of this warm carnival lay not far away from her across the cold bar of silence.

Soon within the house likewise the rush of the children's feet would startle her ear; they would be tugging at the door, tugging at her heart. And as she thought of this, the recollection of old simple things came pealing back to her from behind life's hills. The years parted like naked frozen reeds, and she, sorely stricken in her womanhood, fled backward till she herself was a child again - safe in her father's and mother's protection. It was Christmas morning, and she in bare feet was tipping over the cold floors toward their bedroom - toward her stockings.

Her father and mother! How she needed them at this moment: they had been sweethearts all their lives. One picture of them rose with distinctness before her - for the wounding picture always comes to the wounded moment. She saw them sitting in their pew far down toward the chancel. Through a stained glass window (where there was a ladder of angels) the light fell softly on them - both silver-haired; and as with the voices of children they were singing out of one book. She remembered how as she sat between them she had observed her father slip his hand into her mother's lap and clasp hers with a steadfastness that wedded her for eternity; and thus over their linked hands, with the love of their youth within them and the snows of the years upon them, they sang together:

"Gently, Lord, O gently lead us

* * * * * *

"Through the changes Thou'st decreed us."

Her father and mother had not been led gently. They had known more than common share of life's shocks and violence, its wrongs and meannesses and ills and griefs. But their faith had never wavered that they were being led gently; so long as they were led together, to them it was gentle leading: the richer each in each for aught whereby nature or man could leave them poorer; the calmer for the shocks; the sweeter for the sour; the finer with one another because of life's rudenesses. In after years she often thought of them as faithful in their dust; and the flowers she planted over them and watered many a bright day with happy tears brought up to her in another form the freshness of their unwearied union.

That was what she had not doubted her own life would be - with him - when she had married him.

From the moment of the night before when he had forced the door open and entered her room, they had not exchanged any words nor a glance. He had lain down and soon fallen asleep; apparently he had offered that to her as for the moment at least his solution of the matter - that he should leave her to herself and absent himself in slumber.

The instant she knew him to be asleep she set about her preparations.

Before he awoke she must be gone - out of the house - anywhere - to save herself from living any longer with him. His indifference in the presence of her suffering; his pitiless withdrawal from her of touch and glance and speech as she had gone down into that darkest of life's valleys; his will of iron that since she had insisted upon knowing the whole truth, know it she should: all this left her wounded and stunned as by an incredible blow, and she was acting first from the instinct of removing herself beyond the reach of further humiliation and brutality.

James Lane Allen

Instinctively she took off her wedding ring and laid it on his dresser beside his watch: he would find it there in the morning and he could dispose of it. Then she changed her dress for the plainest heavy one and put on heavy walking shoes. She packed into a handbag a few necessary things with some heirlooms of her own. Among the latter was a case of family jewels; and as she opened it, her eyes fell upon her mother's thin wedding ring and with quick reverence she slipped that on and kissed it bitterly. She lifted out also her mother's locket containing a miniature daguerreotype of her father and dutifully fed her eyes on that. Her father was not silver-haired then, but raven-locked; with eyes that men feared at times but no woman ever.

His eyes were on her now as so often in girlhood when he had curbed her exuberance and guided her way-wardness. He was watching as she, coarsely wrapped and carrying some bundle of things of her own, opened her front door, left her footprints in the snow on the porch, and passed out - wading away. Those eyes of his saw what took place the next day: the happiness of Christmas morning turned into horror; the children wild with distress and crying - the servants dumb - the inquiry at neighbors' houses - the news spreading to the town - the papers - the black ruin. And from him two restraining words issued for her ear:

"My daughter!"

Passionately she bore the picture to her lips and her pride answered him. And so answering, it applied a torch to her blood and her blood took fire and a flame of rage spread through and swept her. She stopped her preparations: she had begun to think as well as to feel.

She unpacked her travelling bag, putting each article back into its place with exaggerated pains. Having done this, she stood in the middle of the floor, looking about her irresolute: then responding to that power of low suggestion which is one of anger's weapons, she began to devise malice. She went to a wardrobe and stooping down took from a bottom drawer - where long ago it had been stored away under everything else - a shawl that had been her grandmother's; a brindled crewel shawl, - sometimes worn by superannuated women of a former generation; a garment of hideousness. Once, when a little girl, she had loyally jerked it off her grandmother because it added to her ugliness and decrepitude.

She shook this out with mocking eyes and threw it decoratively around her shoulders. She strode to the gorgeous peony lampshade and lifting it off, gibbeted it and scattered the fragments on the floor. She turned the lamp up as high as it would safely burn so that the huge lidless eye of it would throw its full glare on him and her. She drew a rocking chair to the foot of the bed and seating herself put her forefinger up to each temple and drew out from their hiding places under the mass of her black hair two long gray locks and let these hang down haglike across her bosom. She banished the carefully nourished look of youth from her face - dropped the will to look young - and allowed the forced-back years to rush into it - into the wastage, the wreckage, which he and Nature, assisting each other so ably, had wrought in her.

She sat there half-crazed, rocking noisily; waiting for the glare of the lamp to cause him to open his eyes; and she smiled upon him in exultation of vengeance that she was to live on there in his house - *his* house.

After a while a darker mood came over her.

With noiseless steps lest she awake him, she began to move about the room. She put out the lamp and lighted her candle and set it where it would be screened from his face; and where the shadow of the chamber was heaviest, into that shadow she retired and in it she sat - with furtive look to see whether he observed her.

A pall-like stillness deepened about the bed where he lay.

Running in her veins a wellnigh pure stream across the generations was Anglo-Saxon blood of the world's fiercest; floating in the tide of it passions of old family life which had dyed history for all time in tragedies of false friendship, false love, and false battle; but fiercest ever about the marriage bed and the betrayal of its vow. A thousand years from this night some wronged mother of hers, sitting beside some sleeping father of hers in their forest-beleaguered castle - the moonlight streaming in upon him through the javelined casement and putting before her the manly beauty of him - the blond hair matted thick on his forehead as his helmet had left it, his mouth reddening in his slumber under its curling gold - some mother of hers whom he had carried off from other men by might of his sword, thus sitting beside him and knowing him to be colder to her now than the moon's dead rays, might have watched those rays as they travelled away from his figure and put a gleam on his sword hanging near: a thousand years ago: some mother of hers.

It is when the best fails our human nature that the worst volunteers so often to take its place. The best and the worst - these are the sole alternatives which many a soul seems to be capable of making: hence life's spectacle of swift overthrow, of amazing collapse, ever present about us. Only the heroic among both men and women, losing the best as their first choice, fight their way through defeat to the standard of the second best and fight on there. And whatever one may think of the legend otherwise, abundant experience justifies the story that it was the Archangel who fell to the pit. The low never fall far: how can they? They already dwell on the bottom of things, and many a time they are to be seen there with vanity that they should inhabit such a privileged highland.

During the first of these hours which stretched for her into the tragic duration of a lifetime, it was a successive falling from a height of moral splendor; her nature went down through swift stages to the lowest she harbored either in the long channel of inheritance or as the stirred sediment of her own imperfections. And as is unfortunately true, this descent into moral darkness possessed the grateful illusion that it was an ascent into new light. All evil prompting became good suggestion; every injustice made its claim to be justification. She enjoyed the elation of feeling that she was dragging herself out of life's quicksands upward to some rock, where there might be loneliness for her, but where there would be cleanness. The love which consumed her for him raged in her as hatred; and hatred is born into perfect mastery of its weapons. However young, it needs not to wait for training in order to know how to destroy.

He presented himself to her as a character at last revealed in its faithlessness and low carnal propensities. What rankled most poignantly in this spectacle of his final self-exposure was the fact that the cloven

James Lane Allen

hoof should have been found on noble mountain tops - that he should have attempted to better his disguise by dwelling near regions of sublimity. Of all hypocrisy the kind most detestable to her was that which dares live within spiritual fortresses; and now his whole story of the Christmas Tree, the solemn marshalling of words about the growth of the world's spirit - about the sacrifice of the lower in ourselves to the higher - this cant now became to her the invocation and homage of the practised impostor: he had indeed carried the Christmas Tree on his shoulder into the manger. Not the Manger of Immortal Purity for mankind but the manger of his own bestiality.

Thus scorn and satire became her speech; she soared above him with spurning; a frenzy of poisoned joy racked her that at the moment when he had let her know that he wanted to be free - at that moment she might tell him he had won his freedom at the cheap price of his unworthiness.

And thus as she descended, she enjoyed the triumph of rising; so the devil in us never lacks argument that he is the celestial guide.

Moreover, hatred never dwells solitary; it readily finds boon companions. And at one period of the night she began to look back upon her experience with a curious sense of prior familiarity - to see it as a story already known to her at second hand. She viewed it as the first stage of one of those tragedies that later find their way into the care of family physicians, into the briefs of lawyers, into the confidence of clergymen, into the papers and divorce courts, and that receive their final flaying or canonization on the stage and in novels of the time. Sitting at a distance, she had within recent years studied in a kind of altruistic absorption how the nation's press, the nation's science of medicine, the nation's science of law, the nation's practice of religion, and the nation's imaginative literature were all at work with the same national omen - the decay of the American family and the downfall of the home.

Now this new pestilence raging in other regions of the country had incredibly reached her, she thought, on the sheltered lowlands where the older traditions of American home life still lay like foundation rock. The corruption of it had attacked him; the ruin of it awaited her; and thus to-night she took her place among those women whom the world first hears of as in hospitals and sanitariums and places of refuge and in their graves - and more sadly elsewhere; whose misfortunes interested the press and whose types attracted the novelists.

She was one of them.

They swarmed about her; one by one she recognized them: the woman who unable to bear up under her tragedy soon sinks into eternity - or walks into it; the woman who disappears from the scene and somewhere under another name or with another lot lives on - devoting herself to memory or to forgetfulness; the woman who stays on in the house, giving to the world no sign for the sake of everything else that still remains to her but living apart - on the other side of the locked door; the woman who stays on without locking the door, half-hating, half-loving - the accepted and rejected compromise; the woman who welcomes the end of the love-drama as the beginning of peace and the cessation of annoyances; the woman who begins to act her tragedy to servants and children and acquaintances - reaping sympathy for herself and sowing ruin and torture - for him; the woman who drops the care of house, ends his comforts, thus forcing the sharp reminder of her value as at least an investment toward his general well-being; the woman who endeavors to rekindle dying coals by fanning them with fresh fascinations; the woman who plays upon jealousy and touches the male instinct to keep one's own though little prized lest another acquire it and prize it more; the woman who sets a watch to discover the other woman: they swarmed about her, she identified each.

And she dismissed them. They brought her no aid; she shrank from their companionship; a strange dread moved her lest *they* should discover *her*. One only she detached from the throng and for a while withdrew with her into a kind of dual solitude: the woman who when so rejected turns to another man - the man who is waiting somewhere near.

The man *she* turned to, who for years had hovered near, was the country doctor, her husband's tried and closest friend, whose children were asleep upstairs with her children. During all these years *her* secret had been - the doctor. When she had come as a bride into that neighborhood, he, her husband's senior by several years, was already well established in his practice. He had attended her at the birth of her first child; never afterwards. As time passed, she had discovered that he loved her; she could never have him again. This had dealt his professional reputation a wound, but he understood, and he welcomed the wound.

Many a night, lying awake near her window, through which noises from the turnpike plainly reached her, all earthly happiness asleep alongside her, she could hear the doctor's buggy passing on its way to some patient, or on its return from the town where he had patients also. Many a time she had heard it stop at the front gate: the road of his life there turned in to her. There were nights of pitch darkness and beating rain; and sometimes on these she had to know that he was out there.

Long she sat in the shadow of her room, looking towards the bed where her husband slept, but sending the dallying vision toward the doctor. He would be at the Christmas party; she would be dancing with him.

Clouds and darkness descended upon the plain of life and enveloped it. She groped her way, torn and wounded, downward along the old lost human paths.

The endless night scarcely moved on.

*   *   *   *   *

She was wearied out, she was exhausted. There is anger of such intensity that it scorches and shrivels away the very temptations that are its fuel; nothing can long survive the blast of that white flame, and being unfed, it dies out. Moreover, it is the destiny of a portion of mankind that they are enjoined by their very nobility from winning low battles; these always go against them: the only victories for them are won when they are leading the higher forces of human nature in life's upward conflicts.

She was weary, she was exhausted; there was in her for a while neither moral light nor moral darkness. Her consciousness lay like a boundless plain on which nothing is visible. She had passed into a great calm; and slowly there was borne across her spirit a clearness that is like the radiance of the storm-winged sky.

And now in this calm, in this clearness, two small white figures appeared - her children. Hitherto the energies of her mind had grappled with the problem of her future; now memories began - memories that decide more perhaps than anything else for us. And memories began with her children.

She arose without making any noise, took her candle, and screening it with the palm of her hand, started upstairs.

There were two ways by either of which she could go; a narrow rear stairway leading from the parlor straight to their bedrooms, and the broad stairway in the front hall. From the old maternal night-habit she started to take the shorter way but thought of the parlor and drew back. This room had become too truly the Judgment Seat of the Years. She shrank from it as one who has been arraigned may shrink from a tribunal where sentence has been pronounced which changes the rest of life. Its flowers, its fruits, its toys, its ribbons, but deepened the derision and the bitterness. And the evergreen there in the middle of the room - it became to her as that tree of the knowledge of good and evil which at Creation's morning had driven Woman from Paradise.

She chose the other way and started toward the main hall of the house, but paused in the doorway and looked back at the bed; what if he should awake in the dark, alone, with no knowledge of where she was? Would he call out to her - with what voice? Would he come to seek her - with what emotions? (The tide of memories was setting in now - the drift back to the old mooring.)

Hunt for her! How those words fell like iron strokes on the ear of remembrance. They registered the beginning of the whole trouble. Up to the last two years his first act upon reaching home had been to seek her. It had even been her playfulness at times to slip from room to room for the delight of proving how persistently he would prolong his search. But one day some two years before this, when she had entered his study about the usual hour of his return, bringing flowers for his writing desk, she saw him sitting there, hat on, driving gloves on, making some notes. The sight had struck the flowers from her hands; she swiftly gathered them up, and going to her room, shut herself in; she knew it was the beginning of the end.

The Shadow which lurks in every bridal lamp had become the Spectre of the bedchamber.

When they met later that day, he was not even aware of what he had done or failed to do, the change in him was so natural to himself. Everything else had followed: the old look dying out of the eyes; the old touch abandoning the hands; less time for her in the house, more for work; constraint beginning between them, the awkwardness of reserve; she seeing Nature's movement yet refusing to believe it; then at last resolving to know to the uttermost and choosing her bridal night as the hour of the ordeal.

If he awoke, would he come to seek her - with what feelings?

James Lane Allen

She went on upstairs, holding the candle to one side with her right hand and supporting herself by the banisters with her left. There was a turn in the stairway at the second floor, and here the candle rays fell on the face of the tall clock in the hallway. She sat down on a step, putting the candle beside her; and there she remained, her elbows on her knees, her face resting on her palms; and into the abyss of the night dropped the tranquil strokes. More memories!

She was by nature not only alive to all life but alive to surrounding lifeless things. Much alone in the house, she had sent her happiness overflowing its dumb environs - humanizing these - drawing them toward her by a gracious responsive symbolism - extending speech over realms which nature has not yet awakened to it or which she may have struck into speechlessness long æons past.

She had symbolized the clock; it was the wooden God of Hours; she had often feigned that it might be propitiated; and opening the door of it she would pin inside the walls little clusters of blossoms as votive offerings: if it would only move faster and bring him home! The usual hour of his return from college was three in the afternoon. She had symbolized that hour; one stroke for him, one for her, one for the children - the three in one - the trinity of the household.

She sat there on the step with the candle burning beside her.

The clock struck three! The sound went through the house: down to him, up to the children, into her. It was like a cry of a night watch: all is well!

It was the first sound that had reached her from any source during this agony, and now it did not come from humanity, but from outside humanity; from Time itself which brings us together and holds us together as long as possible and then separates us and goes on its way - indifferent whether we are together or apart; Time which welds the sands into the rock and then wears the rock away to its separate sands and sends the level tide softly over them.

Once for him, once for her, once for the children! She took up the candle and went upstairs to them.

For a while she stood beside the bed in one room where the two little girls were asleep clasping each other, cheek against cheek; and in another room at the bedside of the two little boys, their backs turned on one another and each with a hand doubled into a promising fist outside the cover. In a few years how differently the four would be divided and paired; each boy a young husband, each girl a young wife; and out of the lives of the two of them who were hers she would then drop into some second place. If to-night she were realizing what befalls a wife when she becomes the Incident to her husband, she would then realize what befalls a woman when the mother becomes the Incident to her children: Woman, twice the Incident in Nature's impartial economy! Her son would playfully confide it to his bride that she must bear with his mother's whims and ways. Her daughter would caution her husband that he must overlook peculiarities and weaknesses. The very study of perfection which she herself had kindled and fanned in them as the illumination of their lives they would now turn upon her as a searchlight of her failings.

He downstairs would never do that! She could not conceive of his discussing her with any human being. Even though he should some day desert her, he would never discuss her.

She had lived so secure in the sense of him thus standing with her against the world, that it was the sheer withdrawal of his strength from her to-night that had dealt her the cruelest blow. But now she began to ask herself whether his protection *had* failed her. Could he have recognized the situation without rendering it worse? Had he put his arms around her, might she not have - struck at him? Had he laid a finger-weight of sympathy on her, would it not have left a scar for life? Any words of his, would they not have rung in her ears unceasingly? To pass it over was as though it had never been - was not *that* his protection?

She suddenly felt a desire to go down into the parlor. She kissed her child in each room and she returned and kissed the doctor's children - with memory of their mother; and then she descended by the rear stairway.

She set her candle on the table, where earlier in the night she had placed the lamp - near the manuscript - and she sat down and looked at that remorsefully: she had ignored it when he placed it there.

He had made her the gift of his work - dedicated to her the triumphs of his toil. It was his deep cry to her to share with him his widening career and enter with him into the world's service. She crossed her hands over it awhile, and then she left it.

The low-burnt candle did not penetrate far into the

darkness of the immense parlor. There was an easy chair near her piano and her music. After playing when alone, she would often sit there and listen to the echoes of those influences that come into the soul from music only, - the rhythmic hauntings of some heaven of diviner beauty. She sat there now quite in darkness and closed her eyes; and upon her ear began faintly to beat the sad sublime tones of his story.

One of her delights in growing things on the farm had been to watch the youth of the hemp - a field of it, tall and wandlike and tufted. If the north wind blew upon it, the myriad stalks as by a common impulse swayed southward; if a zephyr from the south crossed it, all heads were instantly bowed before the north. West wind sent it east and east wind sent it west.

And so, it had seemed to her, is that ever living world which we sometimes call the field of human life in its perpetual summer. It is run through by many different laws; governed by many distinct forces, each of which strives to control it wholly - but never does. Selfishness blows on it like a parching sirocco, and all things seem to bow to the might of selfishness. Generosity moves across the expanse, and all things are seen responsive to what is generous. Place yourself where life is lowest and everything like an avalanche is rushing to the bottom. Place yourself where character is highest, and lo! the whole world is but one struggle upward to what is high. You see what you care to see, and find what you wish to find.

In his story of the Forest and the Heart he had wanted to trace but one law, and he had traced it; he had drawn all things together and bent them before its majesty: the ancient law of Sacrifice. Of old the high sacrificed to the low; afterwards the low to the high: once the sacrifice of others; now the sacrifice of ourselves; but always in ourselves of the lower to the higher in order that, dying, we may live.

With this law he had made his story a story of the world.

The star on the Tree bore it back to Chaldæa; the candle bore it to ancient Persia; the cross bore it to the Nile and Isis and Osiris; the dove bore it to Syria; the bell bore it to Confucius; the drum bore it to Buddha; the drinking horn to Greece; the tinsel to Romulus and Rome; the doll to Abraham and Isaac; the masks to Gaul; the mistletoe to Britain, - and all brought it to Christ, - Christ the latest world-ideal of sacrifice that is self-sacrifice and of the giving of all for all.

The story was for herself, he had said, and for himself.

Himself! Here at last all her pain and wandering of this night ended: at the bottom of her wound where rankled *his problem.*

From this problem she had most shrunk and into this she now entered: She sacrificed herself in him! She laid upon herself his temptation and his struggle.

* * * * *

Taking her candle, she passed back into her bedroom and screened it where she had screened it before; then went into his bedroom.

She put her wedding ring on again with blanched lips. She went to his bedside, and drawing to the pillow the chair on which his clothes were piled, sat down and laid her face over on it; and there in that shrine of feeling where speech is formed, but whence it never issues, she made her last communion with him:

"You, to whom I gave my youth and all that youth could mean to me; whose children I have borne and nurtured at my breast - all of whose eyes I have seen open and the eyes of some of whom I have closed; husband of my girlhood, loved as no woman ever loved the man who took her home; strength and laughter of his house; helper of what is best in me; my defender against things in myself that I cannot govern; pathfinder of my future; rock of the ebbing years! Though my hair turn white as driven snow and flesh wither to the bone, I shall never cease to be the flame that you yourself have kindled.

"But never again to you! Let the stillness of nature fall where there must be stillness! Peace come with its peace! And the room which heard our whisperings of the night, let it be the Room of the Silences the Long Silences! Adieu, cross of living fire that I have so clung to! - Adieu! - Adieu! - Adieu! - Adieu!"

She remained as motionless as though she had fallen asleep or would not lift her head until there had ebbed out of her life upon his pillow the last drop of things that must go.

She there - her whitening head buried on his pillow: it was Life's Calvary of the Snows.

The dawn found her sitting in the darkest corner of the room, and there it brightened about her desolately. The moment drew near when she must awaken him; the ordeal of their meeting must be over before the children rushed downstairs or the servants knocked.

She had plaited her hair in two heavy braids, and down each braid the gray told its story through the black. And she had brushed it frankly away from brow and temples so that the contour of her head - one of nature's noblest - was seen in its simplicity. It is thus that the women of her land sometimes prepare themselves at the ceremony of their baptism into a new life.

She had put on a plain night-dress, and her face and shoulders rising out of this had the austerity of marble - exempt not from ruin, but exempt from lesser mutation. She looked down at her wrists once and made a little instinctive movement with her fingers as if to hide them under the sleeves.

Then she approached the bed. As she did so, she turned back midway and quickly stretched her arms toward the wall as though to flee to it. Then she drew nearer, a new pitiful fear of him in her eyes - the look of the rejected.

So she stood an instant and then she reclined on the edge of the bed, resting on one elbow and looking down at him.

For years her first words to him on this day had been the world's best greeting:

"A Merry Christmas!"

She tried to summon the words to her lips and have them ready.

At the pressure of her body on the bed he opened his eyes and instantly looked to see what the whole truth was: how she had come out of it all, what their life was to be henceforth, what their future would be worth. But at the sight of her so changed - something so gone out of her forever - with a quick cry he reached his arms for her. She struggled to get away from him; but he, winding his arms shelteringly about the youth-shorn head, drew her face close down against his face. She caught at one of the braids of her hair and threw it across her eyes, and then silent convulsive sobs rent and tore her, tore her. The torrent of her tears raining down into his tears.

Tears not for Life's faults but for Life when there are no faults. They locked in each other's arms - trying to save each other on Nature's vast lonely, tossing, uncaring sea.

The rush of children's feet was heard in the hall and there was smothered laughter at the door and the soft turning of the knob.

It was Christmas Morning.

*   *   *   *   *

The sun rose golden and gathering up its gold threw it forward over the gladness of the Shield. The farmhouse - such as the poet had sung of when he could not help singing of American home life - looked out from under its winter roof with the cheeriness of a human traveller who laughs at the snow on his hat and shoulders. Smoke poured out of its chimneys, bespeaking brisk fires for festive purposes. The oak tree beside it stood quieted of its moaning and tossing.

Soon after sunrise a soul of passion on scarlet wings, rising out of the snow-bowed shrubbery, flew up to a topmost twig of the oak; and sitting there with its breast to the gorgeous sun scanned for a little while that landscape of ice. It was beyond its intelligence to understand how nature could create it for Summer and then take Summer away. Its wisdom could only have ended in wonderment that a sun so true could shine on a world so false.

Frolicking servants fell to work, sweeping porches and shovelling paths. After breakfast a heavy-set, middle-aged man, his face red with fireside warmth and laughter, without hat or gloves or overcoat, rushed out of the front door pursued by a little soldier sternly booted and capped and gloved; and the two snowballed each other, going at it furiously. Watching them through a window a little girl, dancing a dreamy measure of her own, ever turned inward and beckoned to some one to come and look - beckoned in vain.

All day the little boy beat the drum of Confucius; all day the little girl played with the doll - hugged to her breast the symbol of ancient sacrifice, the emblem of the world's new mercy. Along the turnpike sleigh-bells were borne hither and thither by rushing horses; and the shouts of young men on fire to their marrow went echoing across the shining valleys.

Christmas Day! Christmas Day! Christmas Day!

One thing about the house stood in tragic aloofness from its surroundings; just outside the bedroom window grew a cedar, low, thick, covered with snow except where a bough had been broken off for decorating the house; here owing to the steepness the snow slid off. The spot looked like a wound in the side of the Divine purity, and across this open wound the tree had hung its rosary-beads never to be told by Sorrow's fingers.

The sunset golden and gathering up its last gold threw it backward across the sadness of the Shield. One by one the stars came back to their faithful places above the silence and the whiteness. A swinging lamp was lighted on the front porch and its rays fell on little round mats of snow stamped off by entering boot heels. On each gatepost a low Christmas star was set to guide and welcome good neighbors; and between those beacons soon they came hurrying, fathers and mothers and children assembling for the party.

Late into the night the party lasted.

The logs blazed in deep fireplaces and their Forest Memories went to ashes. Bodily comfort there was and good-will and good wishes and the robust sensible making the best of what is best on the surface of our life. And hale eating and drinking as old England itself once ate and drank at Yuletide. And fast music and dancing that ever wanted to go faster than the music.

The chief feature of the revelry was the distribution of gifts on the Christmas Tree - the handing over to this person and to that person of those unread lessons of the ages - little mummied packages of the lord of time. One thing no one noted. Fresh candles had replaced those burnt out on the Tree the night before: all the candles were white now.

Revellers! Revellers! A crowded canvas! A brilliantly painted scene! Controlling everything, controlling herself, the lady of the house: hunting out her guests with some grace that befitted each; laughing and talking with the doctor; secretly giving most attention to the doctor's wife - faded little sufferer; with strength in her to be the American wife and mother in the home of the poet's dream: the spiritual majesty of her bridal veil still about her amid life's snow as it never lifts itself from the face of the *Jungfrau* amid the sad most lovely mountains: the American wife and mother! - herself the *Jungfrau* among the world's women!

The last thing before the company broke up took place what often takes place there in happy gatherings: the singing of the song of the State which is also a song of the Nation - its melody of the unfallen home: with sadness enough in it, God knows, but with sanctity: she seated at the piano - the others upholding her like a living bulwark.

There was another company thronging the rooms that no one wot of: those Bodiless Ones that often are much more real than the embodied - the Guests of the Imagination.

The Memories were there, strolling back and forth through the chambers arm and arm with the Years: bestowing no cognizance upon that present scene nor aware that they were not alone. About the Christmas Tree the Wraiths of earlier children returned to gambol; and these knew naught of those later ones who had strangely come out of the unknown to fill their places. Around the walls stood other majestical Veiled Shapes that bent undivided attention upon the actual pageant: these were Life's Pities. Ever and anon they would lift their noble veils and look out upon that brief flicker of our mortal joy, and drop them and relapse into their compassionate vigil.

But of the Bodiless Ones there gathered a solitary young Shape filled the entire house with her presence. As the Memories walked through the rooms with the Years, they paused ever before her and mutely beckoned her to a place in their Sisterhood. The children who had wandered back peeped shyly at her but then with some sure instinct of recognition ran to her and threw down their gifts, to put their arms around her. And the Pities before they left the house that night walked past her one by one and each lifted its veil and dropped it more softly.

This was the Shape:

In the great bedroom on a spot of the carpet under the chandelier - which had no decoration whatsoever - stood an exquisite Spirit of Youth, more insubstantial than Spring morning mist, yet most alive; her lips scarce parted - her skin like white hawthorn shadowed by pink - in her eyes the modesty of withdrawal from Love - in her heart the surrender to it. During those distracting hours never did she move nor did her look once change: she waiting there - waiting for some one to come - waiting.

Waiting.

www.ingramcontent.com/pod-product-compliance
Lightning Source LLC
Chambersburg PA
CBHW051851170626
46807CB00003B/1437